TRUCE 2: THE WAR OF THE LOU'S   1

TRUCE

TWO

THE WAR OF THE LOU'S

T. STYLES

By T. STYLES   2

ARE YOU ON OUR EMAIL LIST?

SIGN UP ON OUR WEBSITE

www.thecartelpublications.com

OR TEXT THE WORD: CARTELBOOKS TO

22828

FOR PRIZES, CONTESTS, ETC.

CHECK OUT OTHER TITLES BY THE CARTEL
PUBLICATIONS

By T. STYLES

4

WWW.THECARTELPUBLICATIONS.COM

TRUCE 2: THE WAR OF THE LOU'S

By

T. STYLES

PUBLISHER'S NOTE:
This book is a work of fiction. Names,
characters, businesses,
Organizations, places, events and incidents
are the product of the
Author's imagination or are used fictionally.
Any resemblance of
Actual persons, living or dead, events, or
locales are entirely coincidental.

ISBN 10: 1948373351
ISBN 13: 978-1948373357

Cover Design: Book Slut Girl
First Edition
Printed in the United States of America

WAR
Series
in Order

War

War 2: All Hell Breaks Loose

War 3: Land of The Lou's

War 4: Skull Island

War 5: Karma

War 6: Envy

War 7: Pink Cotton

Truce: A War Saga

Truce 2: The War of The Lou's

What Up Fam,

I hope and pray this little love note finds you healthy, happy and blessed. With all that the world has going on these days, it's imperative we do things to remove the negativity. Me personally, I don't watch the news anymore. I also don't surf the internet. I have been filling my days with reading, watching cartoons and comedies and making sure I spend time with loved ones. This helps me to not focus on the negative in the world in order to try and bring love and light into it instead. Every little bit counts. Besides, who needs drama in the streets when you can have it in your books. Speaking of which...

TRUCE 2: THE WAR OF THE LOU'S! When I say I missed these bammas so much, that is an understatement! This one picks right up where **TRUCE** left off and there is no shortness of drama...poor Mason...smh. You will not put this book down, trust me! So, get ready!

With that being said, keeping in line with tradition, we want to give respect to a vet or new trailblazer paving the way. In this novel, we would like to recognize:

PAULO COELHO

Paulo Coelho is Brazilian author of several novels, but my absolute favorite so far is, **THE ALCHEMIST**! I've read this novel so far 3 times over the years since I was introduced to it and I know I'll read it again. It's a very motivating story of a shepherd boy who is looking for his personal legend. It's uplifting and full of jewels. Make sure you check this one out!

Aight get to it!! You will not be disappointed.

Love ya'll!! Talk to you soon!

God Bless!

Charisse "C. Wash" Washington
Vice President
The Cartel Publications
www.thecartelpublications.com
www.facebook.com/publishercwash

Instagram: publishercwash

www.twitter.com/cartelbooks

www.facebook.com/cartelpublications

Follow us on Instagram: Cartelpublications

#CartelPublications

#UrbanFiction

#PrayForCece

#PauloCoelho

#TRUCE2

CHAPTER ONE
BANKS WALES' BACHELOR PARTY
1994

The water was neon blue, as it lapped against the golden sands on the small island of Costa Rica. Although the ocean was calm and rhythmic, the large beach house to the left was flooded with guests who moved their frames to the sound of *Gin and Juice* by *Snoop Dogg* via the embedded speakers in the ceilings.

The many brown bodies dressed in colorful bathing suits and swimming trunks while catching each beat, was hypnotic.

Moving art if you desired to paint a picture.

There were women in tiny bikinis with long flowing hair down their backs. Along with men with muscular physiques, penned so closely to their frames they appeared as one.

Would you believe that all the *freak whoreness* in the room was in the name of love?

It's true.

Banks was in a way, committing to Bethany Wales for life. Sure, the union wasn't legal. Not yet anyway. But for him it was serious business, after all, in a matter of months she would be giving birth to his first son Spacey Wales. And as a result, he was taking himself off the market.

When the D.J. changed the song to *Tootsee Roll* by the *69 Boyz*, Mason and Banks spotted each other's expressions from across the room and laughed. Each of them had a woman hanging on their bodies closer than their linen suits, but due to the song they couldn't be bothered to remain on the dance floor.

And yet, at the moment anyway, Mason had two handfuls of ass cheeks belonging to a light skin girl with honey brown hair. While Banks had a chocolate cutie standing behind him, with her arms draped over his shoulders as she whispered the dirty nasties in his ear.

Sure, the song was a hit for some, but to them it was silly, and they had to excuse themselves from the building.

"Wanna get out of here!" Banks yelled to his friend across the room, while motioning his head toward the steps leading to the beach.

Mason smiled.

And it was done.

Five minutes later they were sitting on the warm sand in their khaki colored linen outfits, Mason in a pair of shorts, no shirt. Banks was dipped in pants and a soft white t-shirt. A bottle of whiskey with two glasses sat in the middle, as if it were a close friend. There was also a thick Nokia flip phone sitting next to them, that they had to man since Bet was pregnant.

From their post, with their gaze on the ocean and the stars, they could hear the music in the beach house had changed to *At Your Best* by *Aaliyah.*

"It's crazy how we were beefing hard a few years ago and now we back." Mason shook his head. "Like we never missed a beat."

"It's wild."

"Yeah, we wasted too much time on a lie." Mason said.

"Not even a lie can keep the truth from coming out." Banks winked. "I learned that a long time ago."

"So how does it feel?" Mason nudged him with his arm.

"What?"

"You and Bet. You a family man now."

Banks sighed. "It doesn't feel real."

"Fuck the legal shit. Ya'll married to us even though it won't appear on paper. Who knows, in a few years maybe they will respect—."

"I'm not talking about that." He waved the Costa Rica air. "I mean, I have everything I ever wanted. Money. Power. And a son on the way. But I don't know…something is missing."

Mason nodded. "I feel you. There's nothing like finally getting what you want in life and realizing it's not enough."

"What about you?"

"Me what?"

"You gonna have the perfect life with Jersey too." Banks took a large sip. "Trust me. She'll do anything for you."

Mason looked him in the eyes. "What if I don't want everything with Jersey?"

"Ya'll having problems already?" He frowned.

"Nah, it's not that. It's just that, I don't know if she's the *one, one*."

Banks laughed. "There you go analyzing shit again."

"Not analyzing. I just know in my heart that everything that looks good ain't for me. All I want is what's due. All I want is what I deserve. And I'll do anything to make it happen."

Banks shook his head and sipped again. "You been smoking, haven't you?"

Mason winked. "Yeah, but how you figure?"

"Because you always get deep when you smoke." Banks sighed and laid back on the beach, his gaze now on the sparkling sky. Loving his attention, the Heavens winked back.

Mason fell back too.

"You can think what you want, but I'm speaking facts. Who says you can't get everything if you willing to kill to have it? That's what this country was built on anyway. So, I'm just following tradition."

Banks turned his head toward him. "Well what do you want? More than anything in the world."

Mason's heart tripped.

If he answered correctly and told him that he wanted nothing more than to be with him, he could crash their relationship to pieces. After all, they had been at war for years prior to that point. And he knew that truth brings conflict to those who aren't prepared to hear it.

Mason didn't want Jersey.

He didn't really want the drug game if Banks wasn't getting money with him. All he wanted was Banks Wales, above all.

Above everything.

"Mason, what do you really want?"

Mason turned his head and looked at him. "I don't know."

He fumbled.

And in that moment, he hated himself for not being forthright. But the risk of losing him was too great to take a chance. Having him in his life as a friend, was better than not having him in his life at all. After all, it's not like Banks would ever submit to his will.

"What do *you* really want?" Mason asked.

Banks looked up at the sky. "To be happy."

"Can you be happy with Bet?"

Silence.

"Banks, can you be happy with Bet?"

They looked at each other.

It was long and strange but, in the silence, stood the hints to all their questions. And yet it couldn't be deciphered into words. Because only time and circumstance could clarify what needed to be experienced. And that was the idea that when love finds you, it takes you, whether you're ready or not.

Suddenly the song changed to *Lately* by *Jodeci.*

"Fuck is up with them and all this slow music shit?" Banks said looking back at the house.

"Answer the question, man," Mason said crawling back on topic.

Banks focused on him. "I don't know if I can be happy with her. Not forever anyway." He sat up and sand rolled down his back like droplets of water. "But I'ma try." He poured Mason a glass of whiskey and himself one too.

They were getting busted.

Mason sat up. Drinking everything in his cup he poured another. Riding the wave of Jodeci in the background, he decided to throw caution to the wind, and tell his friend in that moment how he felt. And if shit didn't go his way, fuck it. He was the fallout king. And so, he would deal with the consequences later.

"You good, Mason?" Banks said putting a heavy hand on his back. "You seem off."

"I gotta...I gotta say something to you."

Banks' heart thumped but he didn't know why. Removing his hand, he said, "Maybe we should go back in and—."

"Nah, you gotta hear what I'm about to say. And you gotta hear it now."

Banks stood up. "Let's go back in. The girls—."

"Sit down, man. We don't even know them bitches like that."

"But they waiting on us at the—."

"Please, man," Mason said with one hand on his heart. "Just...just give me this one time to say what's on my mind and I'll never bring it up again. I swear to God."

Banks looked at the ocean, back at the beach house and then down at his comrade. Slowly he resumed his seat next to his friend.

"You good?" Banks asked taking a deep sip. For some reason he couldn't look him in the eyes.

Mason took a deep breath. "I don't know what—.""

THE PHONE RANG.

"Fuck!" Mason said to himself.

"We gotta answer," Banks said looking at it vibrate on the sand. "Could be Jersey or Bet. You know she pregnant."

Angry as an old head who missed the lottery by one number, Mason flipped the phone open. The force was so strong he almost tore the tongue off that bitch.

"Who dis?" He yelled into the handset.

"Mason, why you ain't call me today?" Jersey yelled on the other end. "I thought something happened to you."

Banks could hear her rattled voice from where he stood and laughed. Standing up he slapped him on the back. "I'll see you inside."

Mason saw red as he listened to her nagging, flapping tongue. And, at the same time, he couldn't help but feel somewhat relieved. Maybe Jersey's intrusion in the moment was a blessing in disguise.

Because lately he couldn't find the words to say to his best friend.

Lately.

CHAPTER TWO
PRESENT DAY

The night sky provided a blanket of black guilt for Mason to stand under as he smoked a cigarette on the side of a building. Airpods dangled from his ear as he spoke on the phone while looking up and down the desolate street.

"You sure you got 'em in your sights right, River?" Mason said. "Because I can't have any—."

"I've made this my life," She responded. "Trust me. Wherever they roll I go too."

He smiled.

Although River had always been in the picture while handling the drug portion of the business, she had since proved how valuable she was to him in other ways. And he saw her as a rising star in his organization.

When Blaire pulled up in her white Range Rover, he put out his cigarette. "I'll hit you later."

"Golden," she said before ending the call.

Pushing himself off the wall, he walked over to the truck and opened Blaire's door. As he moved toward the vehicle, he couldn't help but feel like he was forgetting something major. His only question was what?

Blaire waved him back to the present.

And he winked.

Every time he saw her, *every single time*, his heart skipped a beat. Not only because when he looked upon her face, he saw his friend, the one he knew would never have allowed him to use her body for his own gratification, but also because he saw the love of his life.

And that much was sincere.

Even if at his core he wasn't about shit else.

"What are we doing here?" Blaire asked as she wrapped her arms around him. "I got over here as quickly as I could."

He wanted to answer but the mood was suddenly off as he focused on something else.

As he stood in front of her, Mason frowned and looked down at her clothing. Lately he noticed a trend that disturbed him. Her hair was always yanked out of the way, in either a tight ponytail like it was now, or in a bun that sat on top of her head. She had also succumbed to sweatpants and white t-shirts which drove him mad. It was as if she was intent on resetting back to Banks Wales, even if she didn't know who he was.

"What's wrong?" She brushed invisible lint off her shirt and looked at him. In the weeks that passed it seemed as if everything she did was incorrect and found lacking.

"Nothing." He grabbed her hand. "Let's go."

"Mason, what's up." She pulled away. "Say something."

He frowned at her again. The sweatpants really made his dick soft. "Why you...I mean..."

"Talk to me."

"Why you keep dressing like a nigga?" He was so angry his eyes crossed for a second.

She frowned. "I had late hours at the office and—."

"I get all that." He wiped a hand across the air. "But when we first got back together, you were wearing dress suits and letting your hair out and now..." He shook his head. "You know what, let's just go home. I don't want people thinking I'm dating another nigga."

She was stunned.

Embarrassed.

And sick to the stomach.

"Come on, *son*," he continued dropping insults by the tons. "Since you wanna move out here like a dude and shit."

"No, Mason, I...can we talk in your car?" Her words scrambled like eggs in her mouth.

"For what?"

"I just wanna clear some things up. Please."

"I guess."

A minute later they were in Mason's silver Benz. Looking over at him she said, "Before my grandmother passed there was so much emphasis on being feminine and looking feminine. So, when she died, I was relieved to not have to worry about that anymore. And sometimes I forget how important it is to you that I be a lady. And for that, I'm wrong."

Mason looked at her, out the window and then back into her eyes. "I know this is all a lot to throw on you. Finding out you have a huge family, mostly adopted but family all the same must be tough. But Blaire, when it comes to being a lady, I'ma need you to try a little harder. One of the problems we had in the past was that you didn't want to give me what I needed as a man. And if we're going to work, Blaire, I need that to change." He placed his warm hand over her stomach and then seduced her ponytail out, forcing her hair into cascades. "I mean, you're carrying my baby. So being a mother is everything to me. Don't you see?"

"But I won't just be a mother, Mason." She wiped her hair out of her face. "I'm still an executive who—."

He wanted to slap everything. "Can you do this or not?" Mason said shaking his head. "No more games."

Blaire looked down.

On one end she felt his love.

Afterall, it was on full display at all times. It was in the way he looked at her from across the room. In the way he laughed at her jokes. And in the delicate way he handled her body when they made love, even if she felt she could handle more.

But during other times, the darker times, he would snap. But it was always surrounding how Blaire looked, walked and dressed. It was weird because when they first connected, Mason was the person who encouraged her to wear things a little more comfortable since Gina placed such an emphasis on perception. But now it seemed that the slightest masculinity drove him insane. He wasn't interested in anything that bopped, pissed standing up or leaned to the side.

"Blaire, do you want to be with me or not?"

"Yes." She nodded. "I'm sure about that."

"So, you have to be the woman I need you to be."

Blaire felt dizzy inside as she took in what his words meant. Mainly because she didn't know what he wanted.

"What does that look like to you, Mason?"

"It means wearing dresses..." he touched her leg. "It means wearing your hair out sometimes." He ran his fingers through her curly mane. "It means submitting to me."

"I'm not submissive." She said seriously. "I don't remember a lot but...but my heart tells me I was never that way."

Mason started to lie.

How the fuck she know what she was like unless I tell her?

Blaire was getting full of herself to hear him tell it. And she needed to be taught properly.

And so, he started to make up stories about how demure she was in a former life, but he didn't want to go there at the moment. Deciding that with time, she would become used to being what God made her at birth.

A female.

"You aren't submissive in life, but you are always submissive to me," he looked into her eyes. "And I will never let you go. Ever."

She shook her head. "Why are we here?"

He snapped once and pointed out the window. "Almost forgot, I wanted to treat you for your birthday party."

"Treat me?" She looked at her designer watch. "It's after midnight. Everything is closed."

"You of all people know that the world moves when you have money." He kissed her quickly. "Let's go inside."

It had started to rain as Blaire stood in *Modish*, a plush boutique for the wealthy in Georgetown D.C. Even during regular business hours, walk-ins were not allowed, as the rich loved their privacy.

"I can't believe they let you in after hours," Blaire said to Mason, as her beautiful attendant Alexia ran around grabbing various garments that she thought would fit Blaire's frame. Blaire tucked her cell phone in her pocket after sending a message. "This is nice."

"I know you don't like this type of thing." He shrugged. "Shopping and stuff. But I do."

"I like clothes, but I hate going out for things. That's why I hire an assistant."

"I get it, I do, but I also like to treat my lady sometimes. Plus, whose opinion in the world is more important to you than mine?"

Blaire moved uneasily as she watched the redhead slap hangers consisting of various dresses in her dressing room. It was obvious that Mason told the attendant what he wanted.

Fifteen minutes later, thunder clapped the sky and the door opened, causing the bell to jingle in announcement.

Everyone looked to see who was entering.

In walked Jersey Louisville.

She was wearing a black raincoat that covered her entire frame and black boots despite the weather not being cold enough. Her hair was also pulled up in one of the buns Mason despised. Upon seeing his ex-wife's face, Mason's eyes widened as he approached the door in club bouncer mode.

Grabbing her by the elbow through clenched teeth he said, "What you doing here funky bitch?"

She snatched away from him and strutted toward Blaire who was smiling her way. "Hey birthday girl!"

Their bodies connected as Blaire hugged her. "It's not my birthday yet."

Instead of letting go, Jersey hung on a bit longer, which aroused in Mason the sincere desire to steal her in her left ear. Luckily for all eardrums involved, she released her hold.

"Let me go to the bathroom right quick to take this wet stuff off." Jersey said. "Which way?" She asked the attendant.

"The way is back in your car and in your seat," Mason interrupted.

"Aw, boy, shut up! I'm here now." She looked at the attendant and clapped twice. "Which way?"

Alexia pointed to the door. "Back...back there."

When Jersey disappeared Mason said, "Lock the door so nothing else crawls inside."

"Right away, sir."

He approached Blaire. "Why would you invite her here?"

She shrugged. "What difference does it make? She's family, right?"

"That's not what I asked, B."

Blaire shrugged. "I mean, she asked what I was doing and I told her where I was. I didn't know she was going to pop up."

Mason felt like swinging heads with his fists like he was aiming for a pinata. "Yeah but, I mean, don't you think it's weird that a cousin of mine would cling to you so hard for no reason?"

"She said we were close. And you didn't cut her off when she ran into us at my job that day."

"I know but—."

"Were we close or not?"

"Ya'll were but—."

"Mason, with my grandmother being gone, it's important for me to connect with everybody that was in my life. Even if they aren't blood related."

He nodded. Just as Jersey walked out the door.

With the raincoat a thing of the past, jaws dropped when she strutted out wearing a tight long sleeve black shirt and a pink long skirt with a slit so high it kissed the right side of her pubic bone. She even allowed her hair to fall to her shoulders as if she were about to perform a strip tease.

She looked so sexy, that Mason had to reposition his dick as if he were pulling the leash of an untamed Pitbull, which had disrespected him in public.

But it was Blaire's expression that caused Mason to take notice.

Once feminine and dainty in the moment, he watched as she transformed as Jersey strutted in her direction. It was something else to see Blaire's body mechanics melt masculinely into the chair like butter. Even her legs widened a tad, as she took on the pose. And then it was the way her right hand stroked her non-existent goatee, as she bit down on her bottom lip.

In that moment, she had become Banks Wales.

Banks' attraction to Jersey was the reason he didn't want them anywhere around each other in the first place. But Jersey had made her position clear one night.

"Either fight fair and let me in his life, or I'll take him from you I swear to God."

"Why shouldn't I kill you right now? And be done with it all."

"Because you don't know where Dasher is." She said placing her hands on her hips. *"Pregnant with your child, she is expecting a call from me every night. And if I don't call her, which will ultimately mean you tried to kill me once again, she will tell Blaire everything."*

She had him where she wanted him.

And so, he had to introduce Jersey as a long-lost cousin until all would be revealed. But she wasn't slick. Mason knew her ultimate plan was to fuck Blaire back into Banks, and he intended on doing everything he could to stop her.

"You good?" Mason asked Blaire, tapping her with the back of his hand. "You looking like you getting a visit in the Feds."

"Leave her alone, Mason!" She slapped his arm.

He punched her shoulder.

Embarrassed at how she was sitting, Blaire blinked a few times and sat erect. Clearing her throat, she said, "Um, yeah, let me go try on these clothes."

Jersey clapped her hands once. "I can't wait to see what you—."

Mason yanked her silent.

And when Blaire disappeared into the dressing room, Mason snatched Jersey down into a seated position. She almost hit the floor.

"I want you gone, stupid bitch." He whispered. "And I'm not fucking around either."

She crossed her naked leg over the top, revealing a peek of her recently waxed pussy beneath. "My nigga, I'm not going nowhere."

"And you not wearing any draws! Yuck! I can't believe this shit! Fuck is you doing, huh? Trying to fuck her?"

She leaned closer, her warm breath smelling of mint. "All I know is this, she don't look pregnant to me, Mason."

"Whatever, man."

"I thought you said she was pregnant and when she got far enough along you would tell her about all of us the day after the party."

He leaned back in annoyance.

When he first said he would tell Blaire who she really was at her upcoming party, the date seemed so far away. Now with it being less than a month out he was getting sick to his stomach. In his guilty opinion, he hadn't done enough to convince Blaire to remain Blaire before he told her the truth.

He needed time.

Time that Jersey and Shay were not willing to provide.

"I won't let you have her." He said firmly. "Do you hear me? I'll kill her first."

She frowned. "You're serious aren't you?"

"What you don't understand is this. You been feeling her for some years. But I been feeling her since we were kids. And I've come too far to let that

wretched snatch tear us apart!" He poked her
between her legs.

"Ouch!"

"So, you tell me, am I playing games?"

CHAPTER THREE

It was a beautiful day, but it didn't feel like it. As Mason looked over at Blaire as they drove down the street on the way to Strong Curls Inc., he could feel something was on her mind.

The truth was even though he had successfully willed Blaire into his life he wasn't comfortable. He was five seconds from winning a spot in a padded room. He simply didn't feel as if everything fell into place or that all his worries were over.

On the contrary.

There was always the possibility that she would remember her past and hate him for what he had done to her life. Not just mentally but sexually. After all, how could he say that Banks would one hundred percent consent with the things that he had done to his body?

Or with the romantic turn that their relationship had taken.

"You good over there?" Mason asked as he sank deeper into the seat of his Benz.

She looked at him and nodded.

"How come I don't believe you?"

"Mason, you're going to have to stop analyzing everything I say." She looked around from where she sat. "Let's just go with the flow sometimes. You're stressing me out."

His jaw twitched. "What you looking for?"

"I think I left my purse at the house." She flopped back. "I don't know, but for some reason I can't remember to bring it. It's like I sit it on the bed, pack stuff inside, but I still leave it home every time. Why?"

The reason was that prior to Mason's multiple requests, she hardly ever carried them. But in an effort to make her look more feminine, he purchased her every handbag known to man. From Louis to Chanel, at the end of the day they were all left on the floor.

"Is that the only thing you worried about?" He asked.

"Yeah."

"Oh, because I see you going off in your mind sometimes. And I want you to know I'm here for you."

"I hear you, but that's not what I feel."

Mason adjusted in his seat. "Well what do you feel?"

"I feel like I'm under a constant microscope."

"Blaire, that's going too far."

"Has it ever occurred to you that our relationship won't look like it did before I lost my memory? That the things I did back then, maybe I won't do anymore."

"Believe me, the last thing I want is the relationship we had before."

"What does that mean?"

"I like how you are now."

Mason was speaking big facts. Because if their relationship was anywhere near what it had been, they would not be together at all. Since they were only best friends.

Not lovers.

"Mason, all I'm saying is just allow me time to think things through by myself. It doesn't mean that I don't want us. It just means—."

"You know what, it's whatever."

Blaire frowned. "Fuck does that mean?"

"It means I'm tired of being pushed away by you."

She stared at him for a moment. He was getting more insane by the conversation. "Were you always like this? So quick tempered. Because if you were, I can't imagine how we ever got along."

He was always anxious.

"Nah, you make me that way." He melted into the seat. "You make me feel like I can't do right with you, and it's fucking me up." He pulled into the parking lot of Strong Curls. "And I...I don't know..." He sighed. "At the end of the day, all I want is my wife back."

She looked down and sighed.

Lately it felt like everything she did when it came to their relationship wasn't comforting to the man. Which was odd because she was certain she was going way out of her zone to make him feel good. At the expense of her own feelings.

And shit was getting old.

"Mason, I can't argue with you right now. We have a launch on a new product today and..." she shrugged. "I just can't. I'm sorry." She opened the door. "I'll see you later."

He grabbed her hand.

His mouth opened to speak, but nothing came out. Instead he nodded and let her go.

She walked away.

The moment she disappeared within the walls of her business he exited his car and approached Hercules and Aaron who were leaning against a pickup truck across the parking lot. They had been watching them in the car the entire time. In his mind every force was conspiring against him. Especially Blaire's uncles.

"What the fuck are ya'll doing here?" He asked with his arms crossed over his chest.

Hercules wiped his blond hair out of his face and grinned. "You know what we're doing here."

"I get all that. But I thought I made myself clear. I'll contact you. You don't contact me." He looked toward where she entered the building. "And what if she had seen you?"

"I don't care. Because we thought we made ourselves clear too," Aaron said stepping closer. "Our mother had everything to do with the success of that business." He pointed at the building. "And we have been shut out like we don't matter. She won't even let us have the family home."

"Far as I know, my wife is still putting money in your accounts every month. It ain't like either one of you are suffering."

Hercules shook his head. He wanted his money, true enough, but what disgusted him the most about Mason in that moment was the fact that he had changed his nephew, who had made a decision long ago to live as a man, into a woman.

"You know, I can't believe you still doing that shit," Hercules said shaking his head.

He dropped his arms at his sides. "Doing what?"

"You really treating him like he's a female when—."

Aaron stopped his brother with a touch to his arm. "We're not here for all that." He reminded him. Looking back at Mason he said, "We want thirty percent of Strong Curls. Or like we said before, we will make problems for you. You have one week to comply."

"And trust me, we already know you've killed many." Hercules said. "But there is nothing on this earth more powerful than a man who wants what he wants." He pointed at him. "You've been warned."

They both walked away.

"Fuck!" Mason yelled to himself.

CHAPTER FOUR
NEW WALES HOME

Minnesota lie belly down on her bed, skimming through one of the eight pregnancy books she had sprawled out. Although it was confirmed that she was pregnant, it had been two weeks since she felt the baby kick in her womb and she was worried. It didn't help that she didn't look or feel pregnant, and so no one but she and Spacey really knew.

Did guilt from sleeping with her stepbrother in the attic cause God to take away her first born?

When the bedroom door opened and Spacey walked inside, she hopped up. Holding a pregnancy book tightly to her chest, as if it were armor, she said, "Okay, so I don't think we have much to worry about after all."

He shook his head and walked to his closet. "What you talking about now, Minnesota?"

"The baby." She smiled. "Sometimes it may seem like the baby isn't moving but—."

"I don't wanna talk about that." He flopped on the edge of the bed and removed his shoes.

Slowly she walked toward him. "Why don't you?"

He sighed. "Not now, Minnie."

Her eyes widened. "Minnie? Why...why are you calling me that when you know how much I hate it? It's like you are trying to—."

"I can't...I mean you can't tell people the baby is by me. When they finally find out, you can't say it's by me. Okay? You can't connect me to that baby at all." He sounded like a broken record.

She backed up slowly, until her back slammed against the dresser. "Spacey, everybody has already formed their opinions about us. So even if I don't say anything, at this point people are—."

"Nothing has been confirmed right?" He looked up at her. "I mean, right now they think they know what we been through, but nothing has been confirmed correct?"

She sat next to him. "Why are you doing this to me? I don't understand."

He took a deep breath and grabbed her hand. "When we were there...and did what we did...I really thought we were never getting out. I really thought that the attic would be our world for the rest of our life."

She yanked her hands away. "So, it was a *since I was the last woman on earth* situation?"

"Minnie—."

"Stop calling me that!" She popped up and leaned against the wall. "Spacey, you can't do this to me. Don't do this to us."

"Please, Minnesota."

"What we shared was—."

"Wrong!" He jumped up and walked in front of her. "And I know, I know having you keep secret who the father is, is fucked up. But I promise you I'm going to be there. Just not in the open. Okay?"

"So, you want me to raise a baby in lies? Like Mom and dad did to you. Like they did to us. When they had us thinking that dad was our father when it was Stretch instead."

"That's not fair."

"And neither is what you're asking me to do, Spacey."

He shook his head. "I'm moving back home."

"You're...you're..." Her breath increased as her chest rose and fell, and she felt a panic attack dancing in her head. "Leaving me?"

"Yes. Besides, I have to be with Riot and Lila more. I have to, I have to do right by them. They don't deserve me to be gone for years and then post up in this house with you like I'm in hiding. It's not even like it's our original family home, Minnesota. And the fact that we live here together, alone, gives everyone even more shit to rap about."

"There you go again talking about everyone else. What about me?" She placed her head on his heart. "What about us? And how we fought for one another in that attic? We are all that matters. Don't you see?"

"Minnesota, I will always remember you for what we went through. Nobody will be able to take that away from us."

"Spacey, please..."

"And I want you to know, that I meant what I said when we were together. Had it not been for you, I would never have survived what I went through. And we will always have—."

"I won't let you off this easy!"

"You don't have a choice."

"I do!" She yelled. "I do have a choice, whether you want to acknowledge it or not."

"Why do I feel like you're threatening me?"

"It's not about threatening you."

"Then what is it about, Minnesota?" He walked closer, his height dangling over her shorter frame. "What is it about?"

She looked down. "I...I don't know."

"Be the woman you were when we were in that attic. Be the woman I saw rise when nobody but you and I were watching."

"What does that mean?"

"Let me go." He sighed. "Because if you push, if you decide that you won't let me go, I will stay. And I will be whatever it is that you want. But I will never forgive you for it." He raised her chin and looked into her eyes. "Is that what you want?"

He walked out.

Feeling as if her world was crashing down around her, she dropped to her knees. The pain that she felt with losing Spacey, coupled with losing her father, her mother and her life was making her dizzy.

There had to be a better way.

CHAPTER FIVE
LOUISVILLE ESTATE

Shay and her friend Celeste were in the basement of the Louisville Estate caring for the children. There was Ace, Walid, Blakeslee and Patrick. And the younger kids, 1½ year old Patrick and 2½ year old Blakeslee were on one end and being taken care of by Celeste. While the older kids, the 5½ year old twins, were being taken care of by Shay.

Ace was doing his schoolwork when suddenly he stopped and placed his pencil down. Wiping his long curly hair out of his face he said to Walid, "Why'd you do it?"

Walid looked up at Shay who at the moment was printing more assignments off the computer for them. Her plan was for the boys to be so advanced that Mason and Blaire would continue to allow her to homeschool them even after the pandemic let up.

"Shhhh." He continued to focus on his work.

"If you don't answer, I'm gonna scream."

Walid looked over at him. When it came to his brother, there was no greater love. After all, he was his twin. When things were good, they were great. The brothers would share secrets, talk about their kid hopes and dreams, watch movies and eat cookie dough by the pounds.

But when things were bad, the days for Walid were dark and long, and he didn't see a way out. It is often said that the sins, guilt and pain of parents will visit itself upon the children, unless the cycle is broken.

And in this instance, it was true.

"What you talking about?" Walid asked.

"Grandmother. Why'd you do it to grandmother?"

Walid's heart beat heavily. In total shame, he lowered his head, picked up his pencil and answered the math questions on his paper with quick acuity. "I told you. It was an accent."

"A what?"

"An accident." He said correcting his own speech.

Ace smiled. "I don't believe you." He focused on his paper. "I think you liked hurting her. Because you didn't like grandmother."

Shay walked over to them. Scanning the assignments on their desks, she said, "Ace, why haven't you finished your work? We have the English assignments next."

He smiled in a way that usually lit up the hearts of most adults who didn't know him. Because the Wales twins were above all else, so freaking adorable. They had clear vanilla colored skin and all the characteristics of beautiful children that you would see in fashion magazines.

In fact, when they were in public, people would stop and look down at them with awe. But it was their healthy bouncy curly hair which they preferred to wear long that lured most into their worlds. While Ace preferred his long hair to cover his eyes, Walid like his pulled back into a ponytail, that bounced when he moved.

And when it came to motives and characteristics, they were as different as night and day. As different as olives and candy. Or dirt and water. For, Ace learned to use his fake hugs as a disguise for his bad deeds while Walid used his absence of affection as a way to feel a person out.

"Ace, why didn't you finish?" Shay asked again.

"Queen, the work is so hard for me." He rubbed his forehead. "And sometimes it makes my head hurt." He learned the word *queen* from eavesdropping on the real housewives of Atlanta and had been using it ever since.

Celeste who just heard him say queen rushed over to the table. "Did he just call you queen? That's so cute!"

"Girl, be quiet. He running fucking game."

"He is so freaking sweet." She looked at Walid who was glaring her way. "Nothing like Walid's mean ass."

Shay rolled her eyes at her and focused back on Ace. "That's not an excuse, Ace. You have to get your work done. I'm not messing up my opportunity with Mason and Blaire."

Suddenly he pushed back in the chair, jumped up and wrapped his arms around her legs. Squeezing with all his heart he said, "If only I had some cookie dough, I could focus more and do my—."

Shay peeled his arms from around her as if it were the skin of an onion. When it came to their schoolwork, she wasn't playing. A college graduate herself, she was supposed to spend this time working toward being a doctor. But the pandemic had changed everything and so she evolved.

She was determined not to let any of her education go to waste, and as a result, had filed paperwork to create her own school. Her dream was to start off small, secure the proper credentials and then open academies across the states for young children.

It was her firm belief that children didn't use their full potential, and so she was determined to not only teach them an additional language, but to also teach them two grades above the American curriculum standard.

"You're not getting cookie dough." She pointed at the seat. "Now sit down and finish your work."

Focused on getting his way, Ace ran over to Celeste instead and wrapped his arms around her legs. "Can I have some—."

Shay scrubbed him off of her body and placed him in his seat. His curls bounced and hid his eyes. It was a good thing too, because he was giving her the death stare.

Celeste felt a type of way. "Aw, Shay, let him have—."

"Either go see about the young class or you're fired," she said pointing to Patrick and Blakeslee. "Now go, girl!"

Celeste shook her head and walked away.

Maneuvering his paper in front of him she said, "You have ten minutes to finish this, Ace. If you don't finish in that time, you're going to lose out on recess. And you already know I'm not playing."

"Can I go to the *bathfroom*?"

"Bathfroom?"

"I mean bathroom."

She shook her head at his misuse of the word, believing it to be purposeful and his attempt to be *cute*. Because when it came to the kids, it was known that they were both highly intelligent.

"You can go, but that will still include your ten minutes, so you better hurry up." She walked away.

When she left Ace said, "She shouldn't have been mean to me. I don't like when people are mean to me."

"Just finish your work," Walid said. "So you can play later."

"Nah, I don't like her anymore." He stood up. "Going to the bathroom. Be back."

While he was gone, Walid had begun to work on his English assignment. When he saw five minutes had passed, he grew concerned about his brother. Because when Ace was stressed or upset, on a biological and spiritual level, Walid grew upset too.

When Ace finally returned, he flopped on the seat and looked at Shay. When he saw she wasn't looking, he dug into his pocket. The look of deceit in his eyes. When he revealed what was in his hands Walid's eyes widened.

It was cookie dough.

"What you doing?" He looked at Shay who still had her back turned and was sitting at the computer, pulling even more assignments.

"Want some?"

"Nah, man. Shay said no."

He shrugged. "Your loss."

"You gotta chill before—."

"What you eating?" Shay asked Ace as she stomped toward him.

Wiping his curls from his eyes he said, "Nothing."

Not buying what he was selling, Shay pulled the chair out and when she looked into his desk, she saw no signs of what he was eating. But when she looked down at Walid's she saw the cookie dough. Ace had hidden it in his brother's desk when he wasn't looking.

She picked it up. "Walid, what is this?"

He swallowed the lump in his throat. "What it look like?"

"I knew his little ass was sneaky," Celeste said from across the room. Her assumptions were on heavy and she was dead wrong. "And you thought Ace was the bad one. That shows you how much you know."

"Say one more word and you fired." She said pointing at her. Turning back around she said, "Why did you do that, Walid?"

"Because I wanted to."

"But you were just doing your—."

"Man, I ain't got time for all the stuff you talking." He folded his arms over his chest tightly. "Am I going in time out or what?"

She could fully see that Walid was taking the blame, but she didn't believe he was responsible.

Lowering her height, she said, "Walid, I know Ace is your brother. And I know you love him. But you shouldn't be taking the blame for something you didn't do." She touched his leg. "So, tell me the truth. Did you take this cookie dough out of the fridge or was it Ace?"

Instead of answering, he pushed back angrily in his seat. Stomping toward the corner where they stood when they were disobedient, he propped up with his back in their direction.

When she looked down at Ace his assignment was complete, and Walid's was not done. Ace had swapped the worksheets. "I'm finished." Ace announced. "Can I go play now since my brother being bad?" He smiled, showing every tooth.

CHAPTER SIX

It was a beautiful day as a cool breeze invited itself to the dinner that Mason and Blaire were having on the deck of the Louisville Estate, overlooking the acres of lush green land. They were enjoying a succulent meal that consisted of a taco salad with ground turkey, salsa and the freshest seasonings. A bottle of expensive burgundy wine topped the evening.

"...I always knew something was off when I lived at the Petit Estate, but not to the extent of where things are now." She sat her fork down and looked across the table at him. The sun hit the wine glass and caused it to sparkle ever so gently. "Mason, why did Spacey call me Pops when I first let them out of the attic? I never got an answer from you."

Mason almost choked on his food.

"Are you okay?" She asked rising from the table to tap his back.

He raised a hand. "I'm fine..." He coughed again. "Just went down the wrong pipe that's all." *Cough. Cough. Hack. Cough.*

She remained standing. "Are you sure?"

"Yes."

Slowly she reclaimed her seat. "Why did he call me Pops?"

He sighed. "It's funny actually."

"Well I like to laugh." She took a sip. "So, tell me the joke."

"All of my children, Spacey and Minnesota included, used to clown you because you used to have an infinity for the breakfast cereal that popped when you put milk on it. I forget the name of it." He shook his head. "You liked it so much, you didn't even eat it just at breakfast. You had to have it all hours of the night too."

She smiled. "Really? That doesn't sound like me."

"All true." He lied.

"So strange because I can't stand sugary cereal now."

He shrugged. "Things change, Blaire." He grabbed his wine and sipped slowly. "They always do." He sat his glass down.

She nodded. "Mason, what kind of person was I? I mean *really*? I can never get enough of learning about myself."

He moved uneasily. "Why do we always have to dip into the past? Can't we for once ground ourselves in the present? At least that's what you used to tell me."

"I don't know why. I guess I never got a firm answer from you. Because instead of indulging me, you do just what you're doing now."

He leaned back in his seat and dragged a hand down his face. "You were kind. Innocent. And sweet."

"Why doesn't that sound like me?"

"I'm confused, are you asking or you telling me?" He pointed at himself. "I'm just saying."

"Mason..."

"Seriously," he shrugged so hard his back cracked. "I'm the only one out of the two of us who can honestly tell you who you were. And you were a loving friend, a loving mother and basically a housewife."

"Again, that doesn't sound like me." She said firmly.

"Doesn't mean it's not true."

"I feel like...I mean...this may sound silly, but I feel like I was powerful. I feel like I was responsible for a lot of people and so much more." She picked up her glass. "I don't know, maybe it's just how I feel now since we reunited." She took a large sip.

"But lately it seems like I felt more like myself with Gina than I do here."

"I think you're confused." He sighed. "And scared to embrace your current life. Maybe because like you said, you are doing so much now."

"That's your answer to everything. Strong Curls."

"Does it mean it's not true, Blaire? You are overworked."

"I guess not."

"If you just trust me, just listen to what I'm saying, I think you will feel much more at peace." He picked through his salad. "Maybe you should give up some of the responsibility of Strong Curls to your uncles. That way you can free up your schedule a little."

She frowned. "What?"

"I mean they are Petit's." He wiped the corners of his mouth. "So technically they are owners too you know."

"Where is this coming from?"

"For starters you seem out of yourself lately. And I don't know if it's because of the business but giving them what they are due—."

"I know we were separated for a few years but let me be clear, I built Strong Curls from the ground up. Grandmother was running some other version of what I created. Sure, she did the basic concepts and structure in the beginning. But everything else I strategized and Strong Curls belongs to me."

"I never said—."

"And I won't have anyone bullying me who hasn't put any work in at all. That's not how America works."

"America huh?" He couldn't help but think about the days when they moved coke in the streets.

"You heard me." She glared.

"I get it, Blaire."

"How could you? You don't know the nights we spent batching up products to the point where grandmother and I couldn't even sleep. I would've loved for my uncles to be there, but they weren't. And because of it they don't deserve shit. If you ask me, they're lucky to have the automatics I drop in their accounts each month."

Everything about Blaire's body mechanics changed.

She wasn't Blaire Petit. Or Blaire Louisville like he preferred to call her. Nah. Once again she was Banks Wales.

"Blaire, I'm not trying to argue with you. I just—."

"Sir, Minnesota's here to see you," his house manager Morgan said walking onto the deck. She was an older black woman with silver hair that was always put up neatly in a bun on top of her head. Her presence was quiet, but if you gave her five minutes of your time, you would leave with twenty minutes added to your life. She was uplifting for sure.

He stood up. "Thank you." He looked down. "I'll be back." He told Blaire.

When he walked to the living room, Minnesota was standing in the middle of the floor with a small paper bag. She handed him the container. "It's warm. I don't know how much more I can do this."

"Why? You pee every day."

"I'm not feeling good, Mason." She frowned.

"Is the baby okay?"

"I don't know. I mean, I think so."

"So, when are you going to tell us who the father is, Minnesota?"

"Mason, I don't like your tone."

"I'm just asking."

"Well who is the father of the fake baby you got my mother thinking she carrying around? Since we asking questions and shit."

"Minnesota."

"Don't Minnesota me! How long are you going to fake like she's going to have your child? How long are you going to put on like we are your children instead of hers? Like I said, I don't have a problem with her being female. But I need her in my life right now. I'm going through a lot. And what you asking me to do by tricking her is wrong—."

"Mason,"

His heart dropped when he turned around and saw Blaire standing behind him. How much had she heard? What did she think of him now, and all the lies? His world began to swirl as the thought of losing her forever hit him like a bullet to the temple.

"Y...yes." He said to Blaire.

"Why didn't you invite Minnesota outside for some food?"

He exhaled deeply having experienced the exhilarating feeling of relief. "She doesn't have time for all that."

"Maybe not but I want her around." Blaire continued. "After all, everybody has a few minutes for family, right?" She said to him while looking at Minnesota with a smile on her face.

Upon hearing her words, Minnesota lit up inside. It was tough pretending that Mason was her father but unlike Shay and Spacey, she liked the idea of Blaire being a woman now. And hoped things would stay the same with their relationship, with a few tweaks. Just as long as with time, she became aware that Minnesota Wales was not only her child, but also her flesh and blood.

"She can't stay long. She got some place to be. Don't you, Minnesota?"

"Minnie...can you stay?" Blaire asked.

The moment she said *Minnie*, Minnesota's knees buckled. The name used to annoy her to no end. But hearing her say it made her realize that the moniker always represented love.

"Ummmm....I...I..."

Blaire walked up to Minnesota. "I know I don't remember you."

"It's okay..."

"No listen." She tucked Minnesota's hair behind her ear and rubbed her arms as if trying to warm her up. "I know I don't remember you, but you should come by more. I want to spend time with you. Okay?"

Her touch and her attention, in that moment meant everything to Minnesota. Her life was a wreck. She was going through a taboo situation with Spacey and she needed someone to care about her.

She needed someone to be there for her.

She had been praying to God all night for an answer. Was this a part of His plan?

"Okay, okay," she nodded before crying and hugging her tightly. "I'll come by more often."

Blaire held onto her for as long as Minnesota desired, which sent Mason's brain in a flurry of different directions. The last thing he needed was them holding each other into the past, which would cause him to lose his wife.

And so, he stuffed the bag filled with pregnant urine in the back of his pants and as if he were separating the largest shell from the body of a crab, he pried them apart with extreme force.

"Okay, Minnesota, we'll see you later." Mason said, while looking like a madman.

"Mason!" Blaire yelled. "What is going on with you?"

"No, it's okay." Minnesota sniffled and wiped her nose with the back of her hand. "I...I have to get out of here."

Mason nodded with relief. "Cool." He didn't care where she went, he just wanted her the fuck up out the house.

"I'll be by when I can."

When she left Blaire said, "What was that?"

"What you talking about now?" He crossed his arms over his chest.

"The girl was broken, and you tossed her out. Why would you do that?"

"She knows I ain't mean no harm by it. Plus she gets what the plan is."

"What does that mean?"

"It means you don't need to be around all the drama right now." He sighed. "I'm keeping things calm for you."

She stared at him. It was a long stare. The kind of stare that could make a liar uncomfortable. The kind of stare that could make a liar feel a type of way. And as a result, he felt like he was under the microscope.

"What is it now?"

"You're lying to me about something, Mason. And the more I spend time with you, the more I start to believe it's true."

He frowned. "What?" *Crossed arms.* "I ain't..." *Uncrossed arms.* "I mean...you need to..." *Paced in place.* "Stop tripping."

She shook her head. "I'm going to get my hair done with Jersey."

"With Jersey?"

"Yeah."

He stepped closer. "Listen, I gotta tell you something about my cousin. Because this is getting out of hand."

She shrugged. "Okay, I'm listening."

"She's sneaky."

"Is she family or not?"

"Of course she's family. I'm just—."

"If she's family then her being sneaky is something I'm willing to deal with. Besides, I doubt very seriously she's the only one conniving around this estate."

"Now you doing too much. I—."

"Like I said, she invited me out and I'm going. That's the end of it." She stormed away.

When she was gone, Morgan walked up to him. "Mason, are you okay? Can I get you anything?"

"Nah, I mean...I don't know."

"Do you need to talk?"

He looked at her for a bit long. "No. Go clean up the deck or whatever else you do around here. Just stay out of my fucking business." He stomped off.

CHAPTER SEVEN

River Logan sat outside of Hercules and Aaron's house in Richmond, Virginia. She had been following them for days and per usual things seemed normal. She didn't fully understand why Mason gave her instructions to tail the brothers, but she didn't care. She would follow him blindly believing she owed him her life.

Five years ago, River, had the life of her dreams. She was working for Mason on the side moving small batches of cocaine on the streets, which she used to put her girlfriend, Flower, through medical school. Some people thought it was amazing that she even settled down. After all, the ladies loved her dominate way and she relished the single life.

In other words, she was a whore.

Besides, she had money in her pocket and was on top of the world. Standing at 6 feet even, she was light skin, tatted on every visible part of her body and commanded every room she entered. She resembled the rapper Young M.A. so much, that she was often mistaken for her when out of the country.

Then she met Flower James and her world crashed down. She was smart and had goals, unlike the hood rats that crawled under her door which she used to entertain.

And so, she gave up everything but the game for her and they built the life of their dreams.

River continued to work for Mason Louisville on the streets while her girl studied diligently to become a doctor. They both succeeded at all endeavors. But on the day of Flower's graduation from John Hopkins, instead of running into her arms after walking off the stage, she ran to the arms of her husband, Corey Lane instead.

A husband River didn't even know she had.

"Flower, what's going on?" She asked walking up behind the young couple as they stood outside the venue where a sea of happy people hugged the many graduates flooding out.

"You want me to tell her or not?" Corey said walking up to her, his arms crossed tightly over his chest.

"Nigga, you ain't 'bout to tell me shit," River snapped. "What you better do is—."

"Stop," Flower said when she saw River reaching for the weapon on her hip. "Let me talk to her, Corey." She said looking at him.

"But we—."

"Please!" Flower begged.

He sighed. "You got five minutes. The family is waiting." He slowly walked away.

"Flower, what's going on, baby? Who is he?"

"It's over between me and you."

"O...over? Did I do something wrong? I mean, was it the hours I been putting in on the block? Because I can get Mason to cut them back so we can live our lives. I—."

"No, it's not that, River." She whipped the hanging gold and burgundy tassels on her cap away from her face. "It's just that I'm not gay. Not really anyway."

She frowned. "Not gay? But...we...you...and I have been together. We sleep together." She stepped closer. "Your body responds to me. So, what you saying you not gay?"

She backed up and glared. "I know what happened between us, River. Don't be nasty! But you caught me at a vulnerable time. I was—."

"Flower, don't do this." She said rubbing her arms. "I know your mother doesn't want us together and that it always bothered you. But you can't say you don't love me. I—."

"It's not about that. It's about me being married now."

"You wanna get married?" She said with raised brows. "Because I'll marry you today, baby. Just don't leave me."

"No, River, I'm already married. To Corey."

River felt a pain she never experienced before in the center of her chest. It was the whispers of a heart attack. "What you just say to me?"

"I got married last week."

Tears welled up in her eyes as she felt the world blackening around her. "Flower, you...you what?"

"I don't love you. Don't you understand? Why do you make me say these things instead of just moving on?"

River's eyes widened. "If you don't love me, then you don't care if I do this..." she removed the weapon and put it in her mouth. "You don't care right?" She cocked.

"Please don't!"

River was just about to pull the trigger until she looked down and saw a little girl looking up at her in confusion. The child had walked away from her family and wandered up on a violent scene. To protect what was left of her mind, River tucked the gun away.

"Let's go, Flower," Corey yelled returning to collect his wife.

She looked back at him and kissed River on the cheek. "Thank you for doing everything for me. But it's over now." She ran away and joined her husband.

After being gut punched in a way she was sure she wouldn't recover from, River was done with life. It was time to commit suicide. Fuck did she have to live for anyway.

God didn't love her, to hear her tell it.

Out of respect, she called Mason and thanked him for everything he did for her. She thanked him for the opportunity, and for giving her a break.

When the call was completed, she went to the liquor store, grabbed some vodka and went back to the apartment she once shared with Flower. Even opening the door and smelling her perfume in the air made her dizzy with pain. She didn't see any way that things would get better. Not without her girl.

Eager to finish what she started with the gun to the head, she was shocked when she bent the corner and saw Mason sitting in her living room. His forearms were on his knees and he was looking her way intensely. "How you doing, River?"

She placed the liquor bottle on the table and walked toward him. "What...how...did you get in?"

"Sit down. You out of line now."

Slowly she sat on the couch across from him. "What are you talking about? I was just going to—."

"You not about to do what you think you about to do."

She sat back. "I don't know what you—."

He got up and sat next to her. "I know what you were about to do. And like I said, you not gonna do it. Not on my watch anyway."

She smiled. "Mason, I wasn't about to...I mean—"

He looked directly into her eyes. "Talk to me. Tell me what's going on."

"Mason, I want to be left alone."

He sighed, stood up and grabbed the liquor bottle with two glasses. Returning to the couch he poured her a stiff drink and one for himself. "I'm not going anywhere. Now talk to me."

For the next two hours he allowed her to open up about her pain, never interrupting her once. She cried. She yelled. She hit the wind. Just the fact that the boss came to her house, just the fact that he cared enough to check on her, made her feel indebted to him for life.

But Mason went deeper.

He wanted to be sure the young bull could recover.

And so, the next day he moved her out of the apartment and into a building his son Howard lived in after he went missing. He made sure she didn't have to lift one box so that she could focus on her mental health instead. While he was also chasing behind Blaire, he called River every hour, and when he didn't hear from her, he dropped everything and popped up over the house.

In the end, he saved her life, because he cared.

And so, she felt like she owed him.

She felt like God was listening after all.

Because of that alone, when he asked her to follow Hercules and Aaron without letting them out of her sight, even if it meant going 24 hours, she had no intentions on disappointing. Outside of a few friends, she didn't have a family. And she didn't have a life. She wasn't interested in falling in love again, and so she never invited a woman into her home.

When females came onto her, and they did frequently, she would find a reason to say nah.

Often to the point of coming across rude. Still, she didn't care. It was all about new sneakers, baseball caps and peace of mind.

Period.

When her phone rang, she quickly picked it up, "Boss."

"You still got the Petit's in your sights?" Mason asked.

"You know it."

"Good. I need you to sit on another location."

"Say less. What's the address?"

CHAPTER EIGHT

T he baby's day was rough. And in his heart, he knew that things had to get better. And so, as Walid lie face up on his bed reading a book, he grew concerned when his brother walked in, hair flopping over his eyes per usual.

"I thought you were going outside." Walid said.

Ace picked up a ball and tossed it into the wall, *just 'cuz.* "Why go out? Ain't nothing to do out there anyway." He danced in place a little but grew bored with performing since only Walid was in the audience. He was clearly hyped up on cookie dough.

"Thought you were going on the swings."

"Swings are for girl cousins," Ace proclaimed.

Walid thought about it for a moment and disagreed in silence. "Well I like the swings."

Ace appeared to float toward the bed. With wide eyes he said, "You wanna do *something else?*"

His heartbeat raised a little. He knew the look in his brother's eyes very well. After all, they shared Jersey's womb for God's sake. And so he also knew that something was up.

"Nah." Walid focused on his book even though the pages were upside down.

Ace sat on the edge of the bed. The back of his feet thumping into the baseboard as he swung them hard. "Come on. It's gonna be fun."

"What...what you wanna do? You gotta tell me first."

Ace hopped off the bed, reached behind his back and whipped out a book of matches. And with a grin on his face, he started striking. Seeing the orange sparks, Walid jumped off his bed and tried to stop him as Ace dropped lit matches to the floor.

Walid was young, but he realized at an early age that something was off with his twin. And he was concerned that something bad was going to happen to him if he didn't slow down.

"Stop it! You gonna burn everything."

"No I won't." He giggled. "It's fun." He struck another one.

"It's not funny. You gonna—."

"What ya'll doing?" Mason asked entering the room with a smile on his face. "I wanted to see if ya'll wanna to throw around the ball outside."

The moment Walid saw him, as he did every time, he ran over and hugged him tightly, holding on as long as possible. When it came to Walid, it was accurate to say that out of all of Mason's children, no one adored him more.

The boy's love was contagious, and Mason smoothed his hair back and pat his back. "Good to see you too, son."

Walid released him and continued to study his face because everything about Mason intrigued him on levels he couldn't articulate if he tried. But in the deepest level of his soul, Mason reminded him of Ace.

Minus the bad behavior of course.

Ace, not to be outdone, also ran up and hugged his legs before releasing him quickly. "Hey, daddy!"

"Hey, son." He said proudly. "So, do you both wanna play ball or ..." Suddenly he smelled sulfur in the air. "What is that, what is that odor?"

"Odor?" Ace repeated.

"Yeah, it smells like...it smells like lit matches." He walked deeper into the room. When he looked down and spotted a burned match on the light carpet, with scattered sticks surrounding them, he picked it up. "What is this?"

Silence.

"I asked what is this?" He looked between the boys.

"A match," Ace said plainly.

"I get that, but what is it doing in your room?"

"I burned it," Walid said immediately, accepting the blame for his brother once again. "I'm sorry."

Mason's eyes widened and in a moment his heart was broken. For some reason he thought the children that he and Banks spawned would be above the drama, above the nonsense. And now he was learning they were, well, kids.

"So, you're playing with matches now?"

Walid swallowed the lump in his throat. "Yes, father."

"I'm very disappointed in you. Very disappointed. Stay in this room alone and think about what you've done." He focused on Ace. "Let's go play ball." With that he grabbed Ace's hand and walked out the door.

CHAPTER NINE

It had been a long day.

While sitting in the lounge within the Louisville Estate, Mason enjoyed himself a glass of whiskey. Finding out that Walid had a fixation for matches burned him the wrong way, because he didn't take him to be the deceitful type.

Sure, he knew that the glares and stares he placed upon strangers rubbed people wrong, but to him Walid reminded him of Banks as a child, and so he understood his need to get to know you fully.

While Ace, well, Ace reminded him of himself. Which unconsciously caused him to regard him with eyes wide open.

This was a toss-up since as kids Mason's menacing name was Walid and Banks' was Ace. Still, the personalities were not the same. He always thought Walid's quiet energy matched Banks' while Ace's gregarious nature matched his.

Was he wrong?

Was Walid the dangerous one?

Mason was on his second glass of whiskey when Spacey and Shay entered the room. Their fixed facial expressions told him immediately that something was up.

The moment he saw them he shook his head. "Now is not the time." He leaned deeper into the expensive chocolate leather recliner.

"Mason, this situation you got going on is not working for me," Spacey said.

"Me either." Shay responded.

"And exactly what are you talking about? Huh? The part where Blare is living her life as she was born to be? A woman. Or the part where you are too selfish to realize it?"

"Nah, we talking about the part where you got him thinking that we are your kids and that his name is Blaire," Spacey said.

"Seriously, how long do you plan on playing this weak ass game?" Shay said whipping her burgundy bohemian locs out of her face. "It's stupid. I miss having my father around. I miss not spending time with him. I miss not getting his advice and—."

"How do you know things will be different if I tell him the truth?" He asked. "I mean seriously."

She shrugged. "What do you mean?"

"Say I tell her she lived her life as a man. Say I—"

"Well, he did live as a man." Spacey interrupted.

"I'm not finished." He raised his hand. "Say I tell her all that, what makes you think she'll be willing to convert back? What makes you think she'll be willing to wear the clothes she did as Banks? Have you ever considered that you may have lost him for good? And that maybe you should get used to it?"

Spacey and Shay looked at one another. The thought of him not popping back into the Banks personality wasn't even an option. So no, they never considered it one bit.

"Nah, that's not happening." Spacey said scratching his curly hair. "Because he is what he is."

"And what is that?"

"My father."

"Exactly!" Shay responded. "Plus, ain't nobody trying to hear all this tired ass mess. Because you said you would tell him after his party and that's exactly what I want to see happen. Or else."

Mason placed his glass on the floor and leaned forward. "Sounds like a threat. And Louisville's don't do well with threats."

"It's not a threat. It's just a reminder of the assurance you gave us to go along with these shenanigans. Because I'm not interested in Banks being Blaire. I'm interested in him being my father."

"Funny you feel that way. Because his flesh and blood, Minnesota doesn't seem to have a problem with it."

"Leave Minnesota out of it," Spacey snapped.

Mason smiled. "Still think you in the attic huh? Playing house with your baby sister?"

Spacey charged forward and Mason rose up. For a moment the two stared at one another as if they were going to go to blows. The problem was they cared about one another so it couldn't pop off.

When Shay realized they wouldn't fight, which she secretly wanted, she stood between them.

"You gotta tell her the truth, Mason." She continued.

He looked down at her. "And like I said I'll tell her after her party. Or around the time she has the baby."

"I can't believe you did this shit, man," Spacey said dragging a hand down over his face. "I can't believe you, you had sex with him when you know he not with this—."

"I didn't rape anybody!"

"I never said that!" Spacey continued. "But you and I both know that if my father was in his right mind, he never would've sanctioned that shit."

"You see, that's where you wrong." He poured himself another drink. "You don't understand the bond we had with each other. You don't understand the level we were about to move toward."

"Hold up, now you saying Banks wanted you...wanted you sexually even as a man?" Shay frowned.

"Yes. I think he was in love with me."

Spacey and Shay busted out laughing before she settled down.

"Listen, we will wait until after the party." Shay said. "But we fully expect you to tell him the truth. Or we will do it for you."

CHAPTER TEN

It was a bit late in the evening to be at a hair salon, and yet there they were...

"...so, I don't know what I'm going to do but he scares me," Tinsley, Jersey's hairdresser said as he took Blaire's mane down from her favorite bun. "I know that I can't trust him the way I used to."

"Do you think he would try and hurt you?" Blaire asked.

"I think he would kill me if given a chance." Standing 5'2, Tinsley was a brown skin adorable gay man who had transformed into a fearful person over the years. And it was attributed to his boyfriend who terrorized him to no end, although it could be said that he had a way of willing violent people into his existence.

And he didn't know how to make it stop.

"Trust is something else," Jersey said as she spun left and right in an empty salon chair across from where they were posted. "You have to have it, or else what are we doing in this world?"

She was opening her mouth with meaningless words, but she had another motive. She always had a motive. Wearing a little black dress, boots and a tight white designer top, she was trying to be *seen* by Blaire. The gag was, she didn't dress this sexy when she was with Banks or Mason in the beginning.

Jersey sighed. "So, Blaire, how does it feel to be pregnant?"

She frowned. "How did you know?"

Oh shit.

She fucked up.

"My cousin told me." She cleared her throat. "You know how Mason is. Bragging to everyone who will listen that he's about to have a baby."

"Oh, well, I don't know what it feels like to be pregnant, but from everything I read I can honestly say I don't feel like I am."

"Well did you take a test?" Jersey frowned.

"I took a home kit. But for some reason, I don't like doctors. So, I haven't validated it yet."

Jersey smelled a fraud. "By yourself?"

She chuckled once. "That's a strange question. Why you ask?"

"I don't know. Mason wants a baby so bad I can see him in the bathroom for some reason."

Blaire laughed. "I guess you know your cousin because he *was* in there the entire time."

"Oh, well, maybe I'll take you to the doctors. For a wellness visit."

"Maybe. But I hate doctors. So, we'll see. I know I have to go some time."

"Well, are you at least happy about being with child?" Jersey persisted. "Because you don't look that way."

"I'm happy he's happy." She looked down. "That's all I can say for now."

"Judging by your tone it sounds to me like you not feeling it, but who am I to judge." Tinsley shrugged.

"Are you in a relationship, Jersey?" Blaire asked, looking her way, and trying to get the topic off of her.

The way Blaire focused on her in that moment, Jersey felt there was a deeper reason for asking, and at the same time, she didn't want to be presumptuous.

"Not now, but I was for a long time."

"I knew it!" Tinsley said as he continued to rake through Blaire's curly hair with stiff fingertips. "You disappeared for years and I felt in my spirit a man was involved." He grabbed the comb and pointed at her. "Tell the truth, that's why you stopped coming to the shop right?"

The truth was Jersey didn't want anybody asking her questions about her personal life. And although Tinsley knew her as a client, he didn't know anything about her personal life, her marriage to Mason or her relationship with Banks. Otherwise he would be blown away with the levels of juicy gossip. All he knew was that she was involved with someone and that's it.

"I stopped coming because I was wearing protective hairstyles."

"Girl, stop lying. I—."

When a loud noise sounded off outside, Tinsley dropped down and hid behind Blaire's chair. Blaire, on the other hand jumped up, placed one hand on Tinsley in protective mode, and the other behind her sweatpants as if she were reaching for a weapon.

And Jersey noticed.

And smiled.

There goes my baby. She thought.

"Blaire, what you reaching for?" Tinsley asked as he slowly rose, after realizing the sound came from a loud muffler. "You strapped or something?"

Blaire focused on her hand and slowly sat down. "I...I don't know what I'm doing."

"If I wasn't sure, I would think you were reaching for a gat." Tinsley joked. "Let me find out you police."

Jersey giggled knowing she was far from working for the government in her former life.

"Come on, let me take you to the bowl."

After washing her hair, they returned to the chair for a blow dry. Still embarrassed by what appeared earlier, Blaire thought about her past life. Maybe she *was* a police officer. Or a security guard. She shook her head after realizing her guesses couldn't be accurate.

Because Mason would have told her.

Right?

Wanting to think about anything else she said, "So, um, Jersey, were you in love?"

Jersey crossed her legs and again she caught Blaire looking at her harder than what two good girlfriends should. "Yes, very much."

"Now this is getting really juicy." Tinsley said. "So, I'll bite. Who were you in love with? What's his name? What's his details?"

She looked dead into Blaire's eyes. "Let's just say he was my first real love."

Blaire maintained Jersey's gaze.

"Wow, sounds interesting." He continued.

"And there will never be another man on earth who I will love as much as I love him."

Blaire's stare continued to be fixated on Jersey.

"What was his name?" Tinsley asked as he combed and blow dried through Blaire's hair at the same time.

Jersey wanted to say Banks Wales. She wanted to let the world know. But she didn't for many reasons. For starters, Banks' name rang bells in the streets, even if some didn't know what he looked like.

Secondly, she didn't want to be the one who told Blaire who he was at this particular time, which would leave her dealing with the fallback. Mason lied, and she figured he should be the one to tell him the truth. And if she said his name, how could she be sure he wouldn't recognize it, which would force all his memories back.

Third, and most importantly, Mason had made it clear that if she ever said the name Banks directly to Blaire, he would kill her. But not the backstabbing death he attempted before, which resulted in her still being alive.

No.

This time he would pluck the hairs off her body and nick her every minute until she bled out slowly.

"His name doesn't matter," Jersey said.

"Well what happened with the relationship?" Blaire persisted. "Why you give up on him?"

"I didn't."

"So why aren't ya'll still together?" Tinsley said. "You over there looking all crazy. What's the tea girl!"

Jersey had been backed into a corner. She had to be smart with her answer. "I guess I'm still here. Waiting on him to realize how he feels about me."

"Girl, you can play with your life if you want to, but I wouldn't. You better go get that man." Suddenly Tinsley saw a cute dom girl sitting in a rented blue Honda Accord outside of her shop. "Hold up for a minute."

"Everything okay?" Blaire asked.

"Yeah." He stomped toward the door. "I'm just sick of this shit." Yanking the door opened he stormed up to the car. Knocking on the window once, he waited on her to roll it down. "Where is he?"

River frowned. "Where is who?"

"I know Benji sent you right? And I don't have time for this shit no more!" He yelled trying to make himself tough, despite being scared. "I need to be left alone! I need to have my own life and I need him to let me go!"

"Hey, listen, I'm not with no Benji," River said in a voice so calm it shocked Tinsley to the core.

"Then who are you with?"

She shrugged and smiled. "Does it matter?" Again, she was calm but firm.

"Well...um...bye."

Tinsley stepped away from the car and walked backwards into his shop. Once inside he returned to the chair.

"Who was it?" Jersey asked.

"Some Young M.A. looking girl." He grabbed the dryer and preceded to care for her hair. "I thought Benji sent her. Sometimes he'll send his cousins to check up on me if I don't want to be bothered."

"Was her name River?" Jersey asked.

"I don't know. Why?"

The moment she received the description, Jersey grabbed her phone and strutted outside. From her point of view, she could see River hadn't left, just changed positions on the street.

With an attitude she called Mason. And when he answered she asked, "So you got a spy on me?"

"As long as you swinging off my wife's shirt, I'm gonna be watching you freak."

"Nigga, contrary to what you did to her mind, you and I both know she is not your wife. And if you want to have any relationship with her for the short time you do, I suggest you tell River to get lost. Or I might be in the talking mood. And trust me, she is asking questions."

"Jersey, I'm—."

"NOW!"

Jersey continued to press the phone against her ear until River winked and pulled away.

CHAPTER ELEVEN

Jersey was in the alley having sex with a stranger in the backseat of an old car. Although she did this on the regular, she was so beautiful that many of the men held onto hopes that she would eventually want to move into a more serious category in their lives. But she was not interested in another man. All she wanted was to have her needs fulfilled until Banks remembered her.

Until he remembered the fights they had before making the decision that they couldn't be without each other.

Until he remembered the promises made in the thick of the night.

And above all, until he remembered they were in love.

When she was done reaching an orgasm after being hit with the last thrust, she eased off the stranger, the limp condom stuffed with his nut rested on his inner thigh.

She snatched some tissue from her purse and wiped between her legs, tossing the napkin on the floor. The experience was frustrating because although the sexual connection felt good at the moment, when it was over, she was always left feeling like something was missing. And she wasn't sure if it was about Banks or something else in life.

All she knew for certain was that she felt hollow.

And she needed relief.

"That was wonderful," he said breathing heavily. "You wanna grab a drink?"

"What I want is for you to leave me alone." She snatched her purse which almost hit him in the face, slipped out the car and into her silver Range Rover.

After taking a quick drive, within fifteen minutes she was in her house. The plan was to get a shower and some rest, but the moment she slipped through the door, Mason had yanked her by the elbow and slammed her against the wall.

Her purse dropped open revealing a box of opened condoms.

He shook his head at the level of whoreism he felt was on full display. "And you claim to love Blaire."

"Blaire? Nigga, I wants nothing to do with Blaire. I want Banks!"

"Well I see you out here whoring! Is this your way of proving it?"

She yanked away from him. "You the only person I know who doesn't use a fucking key when coming into somebody house! What is your problem? Why are you here?"

"My problem?" He yelled with wide eyes. "My fucking problem?"

"Yes, nigga!" She placed her hand on her hips. "Your fucking problem!"

"I know what you trying to do. You think if she sniffs that trout that all of a sudden, she'll want you back. Well I got news for you, she ain't ever going back to Banks."

"Oh, so you, so you finally admitting to it huh?"

He frowned. "Admitting to what?"

"That you have no intentions on telling Banks who he really is."

"I ain't say that."

"Then what are you saying, Mason? Huh? Because the way you posted up in the house, that he bought for me, it's making me feel like you trying to continue on with this show forever."

"Don't test me, Jersey."

"If you think tonight is a good night to kill me, I need to remind you that Dasher will call the police and tell Banks who he is the moment I come up missing. So, either way it won't be in your best interest to act a fool tonight."

He stared at her for a minute. His breathing rose and fell in his chest as he thought about his options. As much as he hated to believe it, it was obvious.

He was stuck.

He didn't want to tell Blaire she was Banks now, because he was certain she would leave him. He needed more time. He needed lots of time. Years if he could have them.

"You're gonna wish you didn't play these games with me." He pointed into her face.

"Nah, my nigga, you gonna wish you hadn't fucked my husband with that shriveled up dick of yours."

"Shriveled up dick?" He laughed once although his ego was touched gently. "Nah, she begged for it when it was thick and hard." He gripped himself. "Just like you did when we were married."

"You must have forgotten that you gave me a script. There were certain things that I had to say to you, or else you would punish me remember? Or else you couldn't feel like a man." She laughed. "So, our entire marriage was fake. As a matter of fact, nothing was real but the kids."

He looked down.

In that moment Jersey wasn't certain, but she felt she hit him in a vulnerable spot. Was she right?

He cleared his throat. "Like I said, all this extra shit you doing is going to stop."

"I want another pregnancy test," Jersey said with her hands on her hips.

"A pregnancy test for what? I haven't dumped nothing off in that trashcan you call a pussy in over—."

"I'm talking about for Banks! I want another pregnancy test because I don't believe he's pregnant, and neither does he."

"You asked her?"

"No. But he doesn't believe it. I feel it in my heart."

"You better stop saying he 'fore you fuck around and say it when you're around her." He pointed in her face.

She slapped his nail. "I can say what the fuck I want when I want. But you heard me. Proof." She slapped the back of her hand into the other. "I need it ASAP."

"Let it go. And all this *single dyke female* shit you giving has to come to an end too. You pressing her too hard, even for a fake ass cousin."

"You already know I'll never stop."

He was livid. "You really don't know how far I'll go to keep my relationship intact, do you?"

"Nah, we all know how far you'll go," she shook her head. "All the way to the point of raping your best friend." She stormed away. "Oh, and I heard about the family dinner you planning. Didn't get an invite but it's cool. I'll be there with a nice bottle."

"Don't come to my house, Jersey."

"My name is still on that lease and I'm gonna be there." She walked away. "Now lock my door on your fucking way out, creep!"

CHAPTER TWELVE

B laire was standing in the gigantic bedroom inside the Lou Estate, looking at her flat chest. Although Mason attempted to connect pieces to her past, what she couldn't understand was what caused her to remove her breasts in the first place. Her grandmother never gave her an answer that was sufficient. It was Mason who said Gina had them removed to go in line with the cancer story, but even that didn't ring true for such a brutal surgery.

So many nights she thought about asking him again, and at the same time she knew him enough to know that unless Mason volunteered information, he wasn't up for questioning.

And that it was best to let it go.

For now anyway.

But the most ironic part of it all, was that the removal of her breasts made her feel more like herself than any other part on her body. Even though it was on the far end of the spectrum, and she still wore breasts prosthetics.

After showering and inserting the breasts prosthetics back into her bra, she walked into their bedroom wearing a red silk pajama pantsuit. He preferred her in short lingerie one pieces, but she fought him on that saying she hated her exposed legs.

Soft music was playing and she knew it was time to fuck. Sure enough, Mason was lying in bed with two glasses of whiskey on the end table closest to him.

"Took you long enough."

She smiled. "The water felt good." She slid into bed. "Wanted to stay a bit longer."

"That's why I go first," he said handing her the glass. "If I wait on you, I'll never take a warm shower."

"It's funny that you give me liquor when I'm pregnant."

His eyes widened. "You can have a glass or two."

She took a large sip. "Where were you tonight?"

"Had to make a few errands. Take care of things. Without me nothing will ever run smoothly."

She turned toward him. "Mason, what is it that you do? I mean, exactly?"

He laughed once. "I told you. I'm in real estate."

"I know you told me that. But why don't you ever take me to your properties?"

He sipped long and hard. Good thing he had an extra bottle on his end table because he would need it to duck and dodge the facts with his lies. And then there was another reason for having a bottle on deck. Although Mason loved the oak flavors of his whiskey of choice, lately it seemed as if Blaire couldn't allow him inside of her body unless she was drunk.

"To be honest this is the first I'm hearing that you wanted to go see my properties." He decided to pick the best building to show her next week. After he relocated the cocaine of course.

"Yes, I want to go. I want to know everything about you." She held the glass as if it were a cup of hot tea and she was trying to heat up her cold hands.

"I gotta warn you that it's nothing spectacular. Trust me." He drank what was left in his glass and reached over and touched her leg. "Mostly rehab homes and stuff like that."

Blaire quickly drank what was left in her glass and asked for another. She could sense that he wanted her sexually, without him even using words.

She was correct.

"I think you done for the night." He touched her stomach. "The baby and all." He crawled on her side of the bed and pushed her backwards. The back of her head melted into the fluffy pillow.

First, he kissed her neck.

And then her chin and lips.

Her body heating up was the only indicator that she was into it because over the months she was tense during the sexual times.

Some would say distant.

And even cold.

Still, Mason was an artist. By now he had learned everything she liked and did those things the most to turn her on. It was the kisses on the neck. The arms wrapped around her body tightly as he pressed his weight on top of hers. The heavy breathing that was filled with unbridled passion in her ear.

Mason did it all.

"Tell me its good, B." Mason moaned as he slipped into her tunnel. "Tell me its good."

Blaire moved a little but had yet to repeat the script he had given her in that moment.

"Blaire, tell me how it feels inside of you. Tell me you like it. I need to hear your voice, baby."

Again, she pumped, but didn't fulfill his request.

Still, as he stroked in and out of her pussy, he noticed her eyes were closed tightly. What was happening? Her body was in their bed. But where was her mind?

He was tempted to demand that she look at him. To demand that all attention be focused in his direction at once. But he couldn't take the risk of her shoving him away. Besides, even though they had sex many times at this point, being inside of her on a regular still felt like a dream.

And the last thing he wanted was to turn it into a nightmare.

When Blaire grabbed his hips and maneuvered his body up and down while he was inside of her, Mason felt her body tremble. She continued to steer him like the captain of a yacht, until a heavy moan escaped her lips. It was the hardest orgasm he had experienced with her, ever.

But why were her eyes closed?

Why didn't she open her lids, so that they could experience the explosion together?

When they disconnected their bodies, he lie on his side and looked over at her with a scrutinizing glare. She, on the other hand, sat up in bed, with her back against the headboard.

"What were you thinking about just now?" He questioned.

She grabbed her glass. The ice made clinking noises and she sucked them to get a taste of the liquor that was once inside. "Mason, stop."

"Stop what?"

"Fishing. I don't have to tell you everything that goes on with me. I need my privacy. Just like I'm sure you need yours too."

"What were you thinking about, Blaire?" He didn't care that he was intruding on her personal space. He had questions. And he wanted answers. "I gotta know."

"It's too embarrassing."

He frowned. "So, are we in a relationship or not?"

"We are."

"Then talk to me, Blaire."

"Can I tell you anything?"

Mason sat up in bed. "Of course, you can! That's what I've been trying to get through to you. I want the kind of relationship where we're also friends. So, tell me. What were you thinking about?"

Blaire didn't speak with him about what was on her mind immediately. She was trying to determine if she could really trust him. But needing the emotional release more than being worried about his reaction, she decided to be honest.

"I was thinking about Jersey."

Upon releasing those words, she would have been better off punching him in the face. Because the last thing he wanted to hear was that she was thinking about his ex-wife. A woman he could honestly say he loathed.

"Why were you thinking about that funky bitch?"

"I don't know." She shrugged.

"So, let me get this straight, I was making love to you and you were thinking about my girl cousin?"

"Yes, and I know it's terrible. I don't even know why she entered my mind. But I want to be honest with you."

"What exactly was this dream about?" If it was sex he had plans to flip off.

"I don't want to talk about it. You clearly can't handle it."

"That's not going to be enough for me. What was the dream about?"

"It wasn't a dream."

"You know what I mean, Blaire."

She tossed her head back on the headboard and looked upward. "It was sexual. And I'm going to leave it at that."

His eyes appeared to cross again. "So, let me get this straight, my wife has come back into my life and now she's having visions of being with another woman. Who happens to be my cousin? Is that what you're telling me?"

Mason was so delirious with rage that he had forgotten that Blaire's preference had always been women. He had stayed so loyal to his own charade that he was losing touch with reality.

"You said I could be honest. And that's what I did."

Mason looked at her for what seemed like forever and slithered out of bed. "You hurt me more than you can realize. I hope it was worth it!"

CHAPTER THIRTEEN

Blaire walked into the twins' room as she did every night, to be sure they were in bed and sound asleep. When she heard them talking quietly, she opened the door just in time to catch Ace jumping up and down on his mattress as if it were playtime.

Caught, he hopped down; feet planted into the floor like suction cups. "Is that my beautiful, mother?" He ran up to her, wrapping his arms around her legs like a pair of tongs.

She ruffled his hair. "Yep. But what are you doing up? You're supposed to be—"

"I miss you, mother," he continued, laying on the compliments so thickly, he drew attention to himself. "You're the prettiest mother anyone could ever have in the world."

She frowned, slightly embarrassed. "Get in bed, Ace."

"I will, just one more hug." He squeezed tighter.

As he continued to work her hard, her eyes rested on Walid's. He was awake too but seemed far too stressed for a boy his age. When she pulled Ace off of her like a tick, and dropped him in bed where he belonged, she sat on the edge of Walid's mattress.

Placing a warm hand on his leg she said, "Are you feeling well?"

He nodded yes.

"You don't look like it."

In that moment Ace felt he was well within his rights to answer the question. After all, they were twins. "Don't worry yourself, mother." He pulled the sheets up to his chin. "He's fine."

She looked back at him and then Walid. "Get up, Walid. Come with me for a little while."

"I want to go too!" Ace sang.

"You stay in bed. Besides, I'm still not convinced about the cookie dough chronicles I heard about the other day in class."

"It was Walid," Ace said. "I promise."

"Sure, it was." She shook her head. "Stay in bed." She tapped Walid on the leg. "Let's go."

A few minutes later, Walid and Blaire were sitting in the kitchen with small bowls of ice cream before them. Generally speaking, she wouldn't let him eat his favorite ice cream, which was cookie dough so late at night, but she wanted to warm him up to get to the heart of his sadness.

But he wasn't eating.

And so, she knew something was really wrong.

"Walid, what's going on, son?" She dropped her spoon in the bowl and looked at him closely.

"Nothing."

She sighed. "Listen, sometimes it's okay to express yourself. Sometimes it's okay to reach out for help if you need it. Even if the person you need help with is someone close to you." She took a deep breath. "Now what's going on? Talk to me."

"I can't, mother."

"Why, Walid?"

"Because he's my brother." With that, he slid off the barstool and walked away. Head hung low and his little feet slapping at the hardwood floors as he made his exit.

Blaire was finishing up her ice cream trying to think of her next move when Shay walked inside. She smiled when she saw her alone. "I didn't know you were up; Pop...I mean Blaire."

"I can't believe I ate cereal so much Ya'll nicknamed me Pops."

She sighed having realized the lie Mason produced. "Oh yeah. That's why we called you that." She rolled her eyes. "Anyway, I usually get up around this time after Patrick finally goes to sleep. That kid talks *soooo* much. I mean, don't get me wrong, I love being a mother. Still. Sometimes you need your space." She opened the freezer and stared inside as if she were waiting on an answer. "So, what you doing up so late? Outside of eating a snack."

"Was having ice cream with Walid." She sighed. "But he didn't seem to want any. Something is definitely up with him."

Shay closed the fridge. "I'll take it." She flopped down on the stool, grabbed the bowl and began eating the slightly melted dessert. "What do you think is wrong with him?" She wiped cream from the corners of her mouth.

"I don't know."

Shay stopped eating for a moment. "He does seem sad lately. It breaks my heart."

"I know. I mean, my son has never been one for talking or smiles but lately he appears weighed down. But I'll take care of it. I have a plan."

Hearing that she was on top of things like Banks used to be, put Shay in a good mood. Fisting the spoon as she shoveled ice cream into her mouth she said, "That's good. I'm rooting for him."

"So, Shay, we never get a chance to talk."

Her eyes lit up. "I was thinking the same thing."

"At the risk of making everything about me, but still needing to know, can you tell me what kind of person I was? From your point of view."

She smiled. "Wow, where do I start?" She ate more ice cream and puddles hung in the corners of her mouth.

"Start anywhere."

She released the spoon into her bowl. "For starters you were smart. You were reliable. I mean, if something was wrong in the family, you always had a solution. You always had an answer."

"I thought that was Mason." Blaire frowned.

Shay laughed.

Too hard.

"What's funny?"

"Nothing." She cleared her throat.

"Shay, be real with me. I will remember you for it later. Trust me."

She sighed. "You promise?"

"Talk to me."

"To be honest, Mason was never the reliable one in your relationship. I mean, don't get me wrong, he makes a good henchman or whatever, but you were always laid back. You were always smarter. You were always more aware. If you were a kid, you would be more like Walid. And Mason would be more like Ace."

Her eyebrows rose. "What does that mean?"

"Mason is very calculating. Always has been. Always will be. You'll find out sooner or later."

Blaire's temples started to throb. She was just about to ask more questions when she saw Shay crying softly. And since the tears seemed out of place for the moment, it shocked her silent. In addition to Minnesota, she was the second one in the family who Blaire brought to tears while doing nothing but talking and giving them attention.

"What's wrong?"

Shay pushed the bowl aside and ran behind her. With arms wrapped around her neck she whispered in her ear, "Come back to me. Come back to us. Please."

With those words she ran away.

CHAPTER FOURTEEN

Mason stood in a garage parking lot in Baltimore City with River who was fully armed at his side. She was also holding two large briefcases as she flanked him. It could be said for sure that she was down with him forever.

When Hercules and Aaron approached, they were loud and obnoxious. The closer they got to them; Mason could smell the scent of vodka on their breath. They had been in the bar all night, without a care in the world.

"So, what's up?" Hercules asked.

"Yeah, you had us come all the way across town for what purpose?" Aaron continued. "This better be good news."

Mason raised his chin. "It's like this. I've reached a deal I think you both will like."

Hercules rubbed his hands together in anticipation. "Okay...we're listening."

Mason nodded at River and she raised the cases. "That's three million dollars. That's more than enough to get on with your lives. Take the money and step off. I don't want you around me or mine. So, what do you say? Do we have a deal?"

Hercules and Aaron laughed so hard, that Aaron had to walk on the side of a black pick-up truck to throw up. When he was done, wiping his mouth with the back of his hand he returned to his brother's side.

"My brother finds you humorous." Hercules said. "But me, now that I think about it, I find you pathetic."

River moved forward but Mason pushed her back lightly.

"I heard of money doing many things to men before." Mason said. "But never did I think it could make a nigga laugh."

"Let me put you in on the joke," Hercules continued. "Strong Curls is estimated to be worth a billion dollars by the end of next year."

"I don't know what you're—."

"WE NOT PLAYING GAMES WITH YOU!" Hercules yelled slamming his fist into his palm. "WE WANT OUR FUCKING MONEY!"

River dropped the cases and was about to pull her weapon from the side of her pants when Mason stopped her again.

Sure, he thought about killing him. To be honest he wanted to murder them both. But he wasn't trying to turn that dark corner yet since

Blaire had taken the honest approach in life. It was bad enough his drug business was still on and thriving. If she found out he took out the uncles too, he was certain she would drop him. So, killing family members, even greedy ones were over the limit.

For now, anyway.

"Let me say this plainly, never yell in my face again." Mason said calmly. "Trust me, that is your first and final warning." He stepped closer. "Are we clear?"

Silence.

"Are we clear?"

Hercules swallowed and then smiled when he saw the hump on River's hip. "Yeah. Whatever."

"Good."

"But we aren't done," Hercules said.

River picked up the cases.

"We need your wife, your girl, or whatever you're calling him these days to do the right thing. We need her to give us 30% of the brand like we been saying from the gate. And if something happens to us, we have people who will know what to do next." He smiled.

Aaron and Hercules walked away.

"Mason, why didn't you let me pop 'em?" River asked. "They were mad disrespectful and—."

"It's deeper than you know."

"And what do they mean by disrespecting Blaire? I don't get it. You had me take care of niggas for less. Why they still breathing?"

It wasn't until that time that Mason realized he hadn't told her that Blair lived her life as a man. But he also decided that he wasn't going to tell her right then either.

In his opinion the past wasn't important.

"My life is very complicated, River. And when the time is right, maybe one day I'll tell you everything. For now, don't worry about it. When I drop you off, just go home to your family."

"I still don't have a family." She looked down.

"After all this time you still aren't dating anyone?"

She shrugged. "Nah."

"You gotta get back out there, kid. You can't let life pass you by just because you're scared to be hurt."

She looked directly into his eyes. At that moment, Flower's face entered her mind followed by her leaving her for her new husband. "I never felt that kind of pain before, Mason. And I never wanna feel that type of pain again." She sighed. "So, nah, I'm good."

He nodded. Placing his hand on her shoulder he said, "You'll always have a family with me. As a matter of fact, come over my house for dinner. I want you to meet the brand."

Walid was killing his video game while Ace stood on the other side of the room, he was being really loud while playing with action figures. When Walid refused to give him any attention, he would get in front of the TV and block his eye path.

Still, Walid refused to acknowledge him.

Finally, Ace said, "So, you mad at me?"

Remembering Mason's word that ripped him up, he chose to repeat it to his brother. "Not mad. Disappointed."

"You just saying that because daddy said it."

"It's the best word." He clicked harder on his game controller. "Because I am disappointed in you."

"But why?"

"Because you been bad. Too bad."

"You were bad too, remember?"

"You lie, Ace."

"You lie too."

"I never lie. Ever." He thought about taking up for his brother and realized he was a liar now.

Still, in the past, he wasn't a liar.

That was factual.

Walid may have done things in the dark, but he never lied about his actions. Even when it came to Gina, he never lied about him being the cause of her demise. Quite simply put, no one had bothered to ask him directly what happened to her.

Besides, the act was so unfathomable that who could think a child would be responsible? And so, no one asked. Because there were only two people on the earth who were aware.

Ace.

And The Butler.

"You know, brother, I really think you should play with me. Because if you don't, I'm not going to have anyone to talk to. And if I don't have anyone to talk to, I'm going to have to talk to someone else." He moved around with palms spread outward, as if he were, well, a mime.

"Who you gonna talk to?"

"Maybe mother. Or daddy." He shrugged. "So, are you going to play with me brother?"

Walid thought about it for a minute. He thought harder than he ever had about anything in his baby life.

"Nah, I'm good." He continued to play with the controller.

With wide eyes, Ace walked up to him and wrapped his arms around his body, destroying his chance to play the games.

"I'm sorry, brother. Don't be mad with me. *Please. Please. Please. Please. Pleassseeeee.*" He sang.

Walid could resist a lot. In fact, the boy preferred during regular business hours to be left alone. But when it came to his brother's hug, he was no match. He simply wasn't built that cold.

"Okay, okay, stop." He shoved him away. "Get off of me."

"Please, please, please!"

"Okay, I'll talk to you."

He released his hold. "Yeah!"

"I'll play with you. But if you be bad, I won't talk to you again. Do you understand?"

Ace bounced his head up and down rapidly. "Yes. I promise. I'll be really good. You'll see!"

TRUCE 2: THE WAR OF THE LOU'S

CHAPTER FIFTEEN

The dinner tables in the Louisville Estate were packed. So many guests were present, that Mason had to bring extenders so that the large party could sit together. Even the kids had a table, which consisted of the twins, Riot Wales, who was Spacey's son, Blakeslee and Patrick. The kid table was constantly managed by Celeste, who was partial to Ace of course.

But it was the adult table which brought out the finest guests and the possibility for drama. In attendance was Jersey, her hairdresser Tinsley, River, Blaire, Spacey, Minnesota, Derrick, Shay and Celeste.

And finally, after way too many drinks, Mason took his position at the helm across from Blaire.

When Mason sat down, and the attendees who knew about their past as best male friends saw them across from each other, in their minds they felt like they were in a scene from the Twilight Zone.

Only River, Tinsley and Celeste were excluded from the past and the families' dark secret.

After the caterers brought the main dishes to the table, the guests began to eat. The entree was roast beef tenderloin, carrot mash with crème fraiche and shredded brussels sprouts with slow-fried shallots.

When everyone was seated and began eating, Morgan walked out with a smile on her face. "I hope everything is to your liking." She looked at Mason, Banks and then the others.

"Everything is delicious as usual, Morgan," Jersey smiled.

"It's true. Thank you, Morgan," Blaire said.

When she left the silence in the room was striking. It wasn't because they were eating the delicious meal. The Wales and Lou families had a tradition of talking with their mouths full if the conversation got busy enough. The issue everyone was having was that in addition to a few extra guests, a lie was also invited to dinner. And most were afraid to speak, concerned that the truth would spill from their lips like oil. After being seduced out by liquor.

"This is delicious," Tinsley said as he tore into the meat. "I haven't eaten anything this good in…wow…ever."

Not wanting him to be alone, River cleared her throat and said, "It is pretty good though. Never tasted anything so rich."

Tinsley smiled. "I wish I could eat like this all the time."

"We have a great kitchen staff," Mason said while focusing on his plate. "That's why I use them for all of my events."

Jersey shook her head. "That's why you use them. I found them remember?"

Derrick, Shay, Spacey and Minnesota all whipped their heads in Mason's direction as they waited for his response.

It was true.

Jersey had discovered the kitchen staff. And Mason, who was in a downward spiral as of late had totally forgotten. To be honest, he probably never knew she found them. Because if he had, he would have avoided the statement all together. After all, if they argued, they would sound more like husband and wife then *play cousins*.

"What are you even doing here?" Mason asked shaking his head. "I mean seriously."

Jersey smiled at him sinisterly. "You really want this to go down? In front of everybody."

"Leave it alone," Minnesota suggested shaking her head softly. "Let's have a good dinner for once."

"What's going on?" Blaire asked feeling out of the loop.

"Nothing," Mason responded waving his hand as if he were God. "Eat."

"Why do you do that?" Jersey frowned. "Blaire will ask you a question and you cut her off. Don't you think she deserves more? I mean, if you ask me, you should be kissing her feet right about now."

"Ummm, I don't need anybody kissing my feet," Blaire said. "Not even sure what you mean by that to be honest."

"He knows what I mean." Jersey said sinisterly. "Don't you, *cuzzz*?"

"How do you know I don't kiss her feet?" Mason rose from his seat and walked in Blaire's direction.

In that moment Blaire could tell in his eyes what he was preparing to do. And she was disgusted. "Please sit down."

"Nah, she saying I don't kiss your feet, so I want to prove it once and for all."

"But I don't want you to. What is wrong with you tonight? You're confusing as fuck right now."

She cursed and everybody who knew Blaire was shocked. Because she rarely uttered lower vibration words.

But Mason couldn't be stopped. Yanking Blaire's chair away from the table he lowered his body and kiss the top of her foot. When his wet lips were removed, everyone gasped. He was so drunk it took the love of God to return him to the head of the table. Where most felt he didn't belong.

"What did that prove?" Jersey laughed. "I mean seriously. You're so drunk you probably forgot what you did already."

"What is this really about, Jersey?" Mason laughed. "Since you have so much to say."

"I don't think you wanna go there." Shay smiled, secretly hoping it would come out.

"Yeah, Mason, do you really want to talk about what this is really about?" Jersey continued. "Or are you allowing the alcohol to make your decisions per usual?"

"Listen—."

"Nah, you listen!" Jersey said. "Do you really wanna go there or not? I asked a specific question."

Heads moved left and right, each person wondering what would happen next.

"Everybody calm down," Minnesota said.

"I'm perfectly calm," Shay shrugged. "I mean, I don't know about everybody else, but I'm good. Let them talk." The wanting of the truth to be free meant more to her than her own son in that moment.

When Ace started hugging people's legs, getting on folks' nerves in the process, tensions grew thicker.

"Go back to your table, son." Mason said.

"But I wanted to get some cookie dough since—."

"Sit down, Ace!" Blaire yelled. "Now!"

Slowly he retreated to his table, but not without giving her the psychotic baby stare. When he rejoined his guests, Blaire looked at hers and took a deep breath.

"Listen, it's obvious something is going on in this family, and I would like to know what. My memory being impacted doesn't mean I'm not alive and breathing. I feel a joke behind my back. And I would like to be included in on it for once."

"You have memory issues?" Tinsley said in a concerned tone. "I don't mean to pry. I just want to know."

"Yes." Blaire readjusted in her seat. "I forgot everything but the recent years of my life."

Tinsley smiled with the look of someone who had a bright idea. "Well, I know this excellent hypnotist who can help get your memory back if you want. She's been doing the work for—."

"No!" Mason shot up from the table with extended palms. "She doesn't, she doesn't need all that."

"Again, why don't you let her talk." Jersey smiled. "She just said she isn't a child."

"Remind me never to let you back in this house again." He pointed at her. "You are too fucking messy for me."

"I'll go and come as I please in this bitch. *Cousinnnnnnnn.*" She grabbed her wine glass and took a sip. "Mmmm, very delicious burgundy. This was an extremely good year."

Mason's brick gaze of hate never left Jersey's face.

"Mason, I don't know what has gotten into you, but this has to stop." Blaire said causing him to look at her instead. "Since I moved in here you've been so wound up. I don't want to do this in front of everyone, but you are leaving me no choice. I still own the Petit Estate. Do I have to go back there just to get some peace?"

"Please don't!" Shay yelled. "This is all fucking crazy! You're supposed to be with us, not away from us."

Derrick yanked at her wrist and she shoved him away.

"Sit the fuck down, yo." He said shaking his head. "The stage is full already. Ain't nobody trying to hear you read your lines."

"I'm serious! This...all of this...is wrong." Overcome with pain her palms met the table as she remained standing and her head dropped. "I won't play this fucking game much longer. I want my father back!" She stormed out of the dining room, leaving everyone stuck.

Shay was crying in the room she shared with Derrick when Mason walked inside. The soft glow of the light showcased the pain on her honey brown face. Sniffling and wiping her nose at the same time, she sat up.

"Do you know I was in the room when you were born?" Mason said picking up a picture of she and Derrick in a beautiful silver frame on the dresser.

Her eyes widened. "No. Nobody ever told me that."

"Yep. Banks wanted to be there since Stretch had been there for all of his kids, but we had been out drinking all night when your mother went into labor. And he was determined not to miss it." He placed the photo down. "Not only did I have to give him a ride, but I almost had to hold him up as he watched you slide into the world."

She smiled. "Wow."

"If your parents were alive, they would probably never forgive me for saying this, but Banks' face was the first face you saw. Your father was on Banks' left and I was on his right trying to hold him up. And literally, when you opened your eyes you looked at him first." He laughed once. "Your father was too concerned with his boss to even look your way."

Her face moved into a frown. She felt the shade coming on and she was ready. "What do you want?"

He walked closer to the bed. "My son loves you. And I know this because since you've been in the picture, he hasn't even thought about fucking another bitch. And believe me, I wish he would at this point. Because you are disloyal as—"

"If this is about Banks, I was mad that—."

"BLAIRE! HER FUCKING NAME IS BLAIRE!" He yelled in her face. "And if you ever get in the way of my relationship again, my face will be the last one you see as you're leaving this world. Do you understand?"

Huge tears filled the wells of her eyes. "Who...who are you?"

He frowned. "What the fuck are you talking about?"

She stood up. "Who are you? This...this isn't the Mason I know. This isn't the Mason who loves Banks. This isn't the Mason I know who would do anything for his kids and family." She stepped even closer. "So, I am asking, who are you? Because when this ends badly, and it will end badly, you will lose everything. Do you want to lose your son too? All because you threatened his wife."

"Wife?"

"Yes! We've been married for two months now, *daddy*. Invited you to the afterparty and everything. And you were too drunk to come. Now I see you were also too drunk to remember. But let's be clear, I am as much a part of this family as you are. My name is Shay Wales-Louisville and I will fight for Banks and what is right. Always."

He dragged a hand down his face. Taking a deep whiskey induced breath he said, "You heard what I said, Shay. Because if this ends up being a war of the Lou's, you will lose." He stormed out of the room.

CHAPTER SIXTEEN

The dinner party was a disaster. And Spacey, who was on his way home with his son Riot, wanted to get as far away as possible from the madness. But Minnesota stopped him before he could go any further.

"Can I talk to you for a minute?"

He had a minute but not for her if he were being honest. "I really wanna get Riot in the car. I think he's tired and—."

"Please, Spacey."

He sighed, walked away and gave Riot to Shay. She needed hugs so she took the baby happily.

Returning to Minnesota, he stuffed his hands into his pockets and said, "What is it?"

"I just wanted to say you were right. And that I'm sorry."

He shuffled a little. "Minnesota, there's nothing to be—."

"Listen," she sighed. "I'm sorry for everything I did in the attic. For pushing you into this weird relationship that I knew you really didn't want." She rubbed her belly. "And for believing that we could be this weird brother and sister, mommy and daddy team."

"Listen, I'm gonna be there for the baby. I just—."

"I get it. I do. Whatever happens will happen and I've been praying for relief. Because I hate feeling like this." She paused. "Anyway, I just want you to know I'm done. And that I won't pursue you anymore." She wrapped her arms around him.

They had a moment.

A long moment.

He hugged her for what seemed like forever. Separating from her he said, "I gotta get out of here." He looked at his watch. "Riot gets restless about this time."

"I get it. Go home to your family. I'm leaving too."

"Going back to the house?"

She nodded yes.

"You should maybe get something smaller. That house is too big to be alone inside."

"It's home." She shrugged. "And who knows, maybe I'll meet somebody for me one day."

"But nobody is there now." He stroked her shoulders. "And you deserve to have somebody there *now*."

"I do, and I've been praying on it." She sighed. "But I'll be fine. I feel it in my heart."

He smiled and kissed her on the cheek. Happy to be done with it all. "Okay. I'll call you later to check on you."

As she walked out of the house and toward her car, she thought about all the things that happened between them in the attic. In her opinion, the psychological damage hit her the hardest. After all, the attic wasn't her first taste of mental torture.

Minnesota Wales had been through a lot.

She had been pursued by one of Mason's hitman in the woods whose sole purpose was to kill her. She had been hassled by her ex-boyfriend Arlyndo and virtually kidnapped while he attempted to take her out of the country. And even the situation with Banks, in which she had to come to terms with her father actually being a woman, who had turned back to her mother who now went by the name Blaire, weighed down her soul.

And then there was the attic.

The attic was the definition of a beautiful dark nightmare.

When she made it to her house and flopped on the edge of her bed and looked around the home, she and Spacey once shared together. She felt sadder than ever and her stomach grew queasy. Believing it was loneliness, she grabbed her phone and reconnected to a dating app she used in the past.

After several swipes, she landed on a man named Zercy. And as she looked at the picture something about his eyes made her smile and she wondered what kind of person he was. After making a connection, she waited for him to respond.

He hit her back two minutes later.

ZERCY: You ready for me to change your life?

She frowned. His approach was a bit thick, but the question was good. She was ready for a change.

MINNESOTA: Been ready.

ZERCY: I can't waste any time. I'm looking for a wife now.

MINNESOTA: Why the rush?

ZERCY: Why not?

She smiled. If nothing else could be said, he was definitely interesting.

MINNESOTA: So where do we go from here?

ZERCY: Meet me now.

She glanced down at her watch. It was after 11:00 at night.

MINNESOTA: It's late.

ZERCY: True. But why wait to start the rest of your life?

Having heard all she needed to hear; and feeling somewhat desperate, she was in her car within five minutes. Her bulging stomach did major flips as she thought about what she was doing. She was a pregnant woman, who was quite far along even though she barely showed. Her move was definitely reckless, but with things not being normal in her family, she needed recklessness to reawaken her soul.

Besides, her entire upbringings were brought up on the impetuous life, and so she found familiarity in chaos and the unknown.

When she made it to the dimly lit park, she was surprised to see three females leaning against the white Prius she was told to look out for. What struck her immediately was that even though they had different body types, their faces were very similar. All three had light brown skin, with wild curly hair that resembled her brothers Ace and Walid.

But none of them were male.

Parking her Benz, she hopped out and gripped her belly which oddly enough, had taken a turn toward the painful.

"Where's Zercy?" She asked approaching them cautiously while looking around from where she stood.

"Are you okay?" One of them asked.

"Wait, are you pregnant?" The second replied.

"Oh great, she's pregnant and cruising dating apps." The third one responded.

"Are you all playing games?" Minnesota glared. She wanted an answer asap. "Because I came here to meet Zercy. And from where I'm standing none of ya'll look like him."

Before they could respond, a 1998 white pick-up truck pulled up and parked any kind of way. When Minnesota glanced at the face of the driver, she saw it was Zercy from the app. His picture didn't do him justice. His golden-brown skin and neat dread locks were pulled back with a crisp design and they looked fresh.

"I know ya'll not doing this again," he said jumping out of the truck. "What is wrong with you three?"

Although his voice boomed with power, there also seemed to be a calmness to his tone. As if he were confronting them while also caring for their emotions at the same time.

The first girl said, "We just wanted to—."

Suddenly, Minnesota dropped on the ground and immediately all attention was taken off of the foursome and placed onto her.

"Something's wrong!" He picked her up and placed her in his truck. "I'm taking her to the hospital."

When Minnesota woke up in the hospital, she was shocked to see Zercy at her side. Concerned, he placed a book down he was reading and stood up.

"How you feeling? You want me to call the doctor? So they can check on you and—"

"What happened?" She felt her stomach which was considerably lower than it was earlier. "Is my baby—."

"Let me get the doctor."

"Please." She grabbed his hand. "Just, just tell me the truth."

He looked down and then back at her. "You lost the baby. I'm sorry."

CHAPTER SEVENTEEN

The moonlight shined through the window as Blaire sat in the tub, reflecting about the dinner party earlier that evening. The soothing warm water coupled with the frothy white suds and the lavender scented oil caused her to drift off into a calming sleep.

But it was the dream she was having that snatched her soul.

THE NIGHT HOWARD LOUISVILLE WAS MURDERED

The dream Blaire was having was from a man's point of view. A man whose face Blaire could not see. Still, as the man strolled deep inside a motel room, when he sat on the bed it squeaked. Other men whose faces she could not see were also present.

"How'd you find me?" Howard trembled.

"I always knew where you were."

Howard's eyes widened. "So, so, you gonna kill me?"

"Yes." The man said.

"Please don't. I...I made a mistake and I...my life was messed up. My, my father ignored me. He, he abandoned me. But if I had it to do all over again, I wouldn't kill my brother. I wouldn't have killed Bet either. I loved —."

"There's no need in crying. My mind is made up. I just wanna know why?" The man continued.

He wept quietly. "I don't wanna—."

"WHY DID YOU KILL BET!?"

Howard exhaled. "Because she was going to tell on you. About what you were doing with my mother."

The man directed his attention away from Howard and said, "Do it," to the others present in the room.

And on his word, the men strangled Howard to death.

PRESENT DAY

The moment Blaire woke up from the nightmare, she sat up straight in the tub. Water splashed everywhere as her breath rose and fell heavily inside of her chest. Blinking rapidly, she uttered the name, "*Howard.*"

Although Howard sounded familiar, she didn't know who he was or why she dreamed of him. And then an idea dawned on her mind.

Could it be possible that Mason killed Howard?

After all, she saw the entire act, but she didn't recognize the stranger talking since she saw the dream from his point of view.

And still, he also felt familiar.

Why?

It was settled, she would tell Mason about the dream in the hopes that he would bring the event to an understanding. After all, the recollection felt so real, she believed it actually happened and that frightened her even more.

After drying off and wearing her silk pajama pantsuit, she was shocked to see Mason standing at the bathroom door. "I hope you won't take that faggy seriously, Blaire."

"Faggy?" She frowned.

"Don't pretend like you didn't hear him."

She glared. "Mason, what are you talking about?"

"That nigga that Jersey brought to the dinner party. The little ass hairdresser or whatever the fuck he was."

Blaire walked past him and eased into bed. "Mason, to be honest, I haven't given much thought to what he said. But if I did want to use a hypnotist, I would be well within my rights."

"Actually, you wouldn't."

"Why are you so intent on keeping me from learning about my past?"

"I'm not trying to keep you from your—."

"What I want to know is why was Shay upset at dinner? Every time I'm around her, I get the impression that she wants to say more than she's allowed. What is torturing her mind?"

He waved the air, something he did on a regular. "That girl been crazy." He walked toward the bed. "You should pay zero attention to her at all times."

Her eyes pressed together. "I don't believe you."

"Whether you believe me or not doesn't mean it's not true. I always speak the truth to—."

"Who is Howard?" Blaire interjected.

His eyes widened. In fact, he looked as if he'd seen a ghost. Instead, he heard a ghost's name. "Who is H...Howard?"

"You tell me, Mason."

He backed away and flopped on the sofa at the foot of their bed. "Where did you hear that name? Jersey? Because you need to stay as far away from her as possible."

She frowned. "Mason, who is he?"

"Where did you hear that name?" He asked firmer.

"It came to me in a dream. Now are you going to answer the question or not?"

"You know what, I really don't have time for this."

"Mason, either answer me, or I'm out of here. Like I said, I still have the Petit Estate and will have no problem bouncing if you keep on disrespecting me. Don't tempt me."

This was a unique situation Mason found himself in. Telling her who Howard was, would open a new window into the doorway of her mind. But to not tell her was essentially denying his son. Whom he believed was hiding from the world after killing Patterson. His own brother.

And so, he felt it best to conceal the truth, until he deemed fit at a later time.

"I don't know who Howard is." He got up and walked to his side of the bed, sliding inside of the covers, he turned his back in her direction and flipped his lamp switch off. Denying his flesh and blood hit him hard and he felt ill. But he would never let her know.

But her light was still on.

And so, she could still *see*.

In that moment, his deceit made Blaire question him even more. And in one instance, with one lie, Blaire decided that it was possible that Mason killed whoever Howard was, and she was determined to find out why.

With Mason's back turned to her he said, "Have I ever done anything since you met me but love you, Blaire? But take care of you. But protect you. Is this the thanks that I get for my loyalty. Constant questioning like you police."

"Mason, what I know is this. You are a liar. And if I find out what that lie is about, I'm scared to think about what I may do to you."

He flipped his light on and turned around. "Are you threatening me?"

She flipped her light switch off and turned her back toward him. "You heard what I said."

CHAPTER EIGHTEEN

T insley was in the passenger seat of River's car as she chauffeured him to his apartment. Jersey had asked her to take him, as she wanted the few more minutes to get on Mason's nerves and to play with Patrick after the dinner party earlier that night. And so, they were forced into a car with one another.

Two strangers.

Bound by their mismatch association with the Wales and Louisville's. And a secret that neither one of them was in on.

"So, I was thinking about performing down the Clouds nightclub," Tinsley said. He was using the moment to break the silence more than anything else. "For brunch. You should check me out sometime."

"Nah. I ain't got time for anything other than business."

Tinsley looked down at his hands and then out the window.

Feeling bad she said, "Well what do you do there?"

"Drag."

She smiled. "I've been to a few drag brunches in my day."

"Do you like them?"

"They were nice. A lot of talent."

"So, when was the last time you been?"

"It was when I...I mean..." River continued to pilot the car and it was obvious that her mood would not allow much more in the way of detail. Talking about Flower still hurt. "Just leave it alone."

"If I'm being pushy, I'm not trying to. It's—."

"It has nothing to do with you being pushy," she sighed. "My girl she was, I don't know, big on drag brunches. And we went a few times for her."

"Are you still with her?"

"Nah. She's married."

Tinsley frowned. "Wow. Didn't take you for dealing with a married woman. I guess you never truly know a person."

River smiled and shook her head. "Yeah, okay."

"Yeah okay?" He got louder. "I just called you on your bullshit and that's all you can say?"

"I know what kind of person you are and I'm not gonna let you take me there."

"And what kind of person is that?"

"You want to argue." She laughed once. "And I stopped arguing with people a long time ago."

"So, you don't believe in speaking up for yourself?"

"I speak up. When it counts."

"Is that why you lost your girl? Because you spoke up for yourself?" He paused. "Because if you weren't sleeping around with a married woman, that means she got married after or while you were together. Either way it's your loss."

Suddenly River frowned. "You shouldn't speak on what you don't know."

"I can speak on what I like."

"Listen, how about we don't say anything else to each other for the rest of the ride. That way—."

WHAM!

Suddenly the side of River's car was struck by a red Malibu. Before River could get her bearings together, the passenger side door was yanked open and Tinsley was sucked out.

"Why didn't you answer my calls huh?" The man said grabbing Tinsley by the front of the shirt while hitting him in the center of the nose repeatedly. "Why didn't you answer my calls?"

Still feeling a little stunned from being struck by another vehicle, it took River a few moments to get herself together. But when she did it came at the best time. Because the stranger was beating Tinsley so badly, he was about to lose consciousness.

Popping her trunk, she dipped inside, grabbed her bat and hit him over top of the head once from behind. When he was down, she struck him once more to be sure he stayed where she flattened him.

Stopping the crime, she helped Tinsley to his feet. Since he was way shorter than she was, one side of his body was hiked up as his arm rested on her shoulder. It took some effort but, in the end, they were safely inside her car. The vehicle sputtered a few times due to the damage before turning back on. Within a minute they were far from the scene.

Looking through her rearview mirror she asked, "Who was that?" Tinsley's head rocked a little and his face was painted with blood. Digging into the glove compartment, she pulled out some napkins. Placing it in his hand she said, "Clean yourself up."

He could barely move his hand.

Pulling over, she took the napkin and wiped his face softly. His eyes opened fully when she applied too much pressure. "Ouchhh. That hurts."

"Who was that?"

He grabbed the napkin from her hand. "My boyfriend. Well, my ex-boyfriend. His name is Benji."

"Well I don't have to tell you that he's crazy. Why would you even deal with a man like that?"

"He doesn't get the picture that I don't want to be bothered anymore. But he isn't always like that."

"So, you cool with how he acted?" River shook her head.

"I didn't say that."

"Because if I gotta do all that to get a person back, I don't want 'em." She turned the car back on. "Let me take you home. Because—."

"NO!" He said placing a hand on her arm.

She jumped at his touch. "Why?"

Removing his hand he said, "If I go back to my house, he'll kill me."

"So, where do you wanna go?"

"Anywhere but home. Please."

When Tinsley walked into the luxury apartment overlooking downtown Baltimore, his breath was taken away. Through his good eye, which was slightly more open compared to the other, he took in the breathtaking view of the city via the floor to ceiling windows. What he also noticed was that the house was barely furnished.

"You just moved here?" He asked sitting on the stiff black couch. "It's nice but it doesn't have a heart yet.

"Nah. I been here for a while." She tossed her keys on the plain wooden table by the couch.

"Why isn't there more furniture?" He rubbed his arms. "It feels so cold in here."

River walked to the fridge and grabbed a bag of frozen peas. "You ask a lot of questions for somebody doing you a favor. Put this on your face."

He did and the moment it touched his skin he winced in pain before placing it back. "I can't believe he beat me like this. It's the furthest he ever went."

She sighed. She was done talking about old boy as she could still see he was very resistant to cutting a nigga off. "You can stay here for as long as you want. I'm never here anyway. It won't be a problem."

"Are you serious? This place is beautiful. The only view I got at my apartment is of a dumpster."

"Yep, I'm serious. You can stay." She shrugged. "I have an extra room too. It's empty but..." She dug into her pocket and removed a wad of cash. Handing it to him she said, "Fix it up like you want."

He looked down at the stack. "I won't need all of this money."

"Use the rest for food." She shrugged. "Because I eat out every day. So, nothing is in the fridge." She paused. "And if I were you, I would stay away from your salon. If he found you in my car, that means he'll find you there. You gotta be careful."

"Don't worry. I never want to see him again."

CHAPTER NINETEEN

It was a regular day in the twins' world and Ace was losing on the video game he was playing with his brother. And since they were on their fourth game, and he hadn't won yet, he was growing heated. So, when he got to a point in the game where if Walid stopped playing, he could win, he grabbed the remote and tossed it across the room.

Using the delay, he made a few moves and just like that, he became the victor!

Dropping the remote Ace yelled, "I did it! I beat you! I beat you!"

Walid wiped a hand down his face. "Why you do that? You coulda broke the controller."

"I won! I won!" He yelled with fists like knots pointing up into the air. "You couldn't beat me because I'm better."

"Nah, why you throw the controller?"

"Because you were moving too slow."

Walid lowered his brow. "Remember what I said?"

Ace did remember the threat to hoard him. He specifically told him if he were bad again, he would no longer talk to him. But he chose to play dumb instead. "No. I don't remember."

"I said if you be bad again, I wasn't playing with you no more. And now I'm not playing with you no more." Walid was tired of his brother getting meaner. He was tired of the things he said and did to other people. All he wanted was some space from him and so he got up and stormed out of the room.

On his way out, his face slammed into Spacey's legs.

"Hey, I was just about to come scoop you and your brother to go to the park." He ruffled his fluffy ponytail. "Riot is in the kitchen getting a snack. You wanna roll with us?" When he saw the expression on his face, he lowered his height. "Hold up, are you good?"

Walid looked like he wanted to cry and yell at the same time. He loved his brother, he truly did, he just wished he stopped being so bad. He also didn't want to get Ace in trouble. When it came to the motto 'brother's keeper' he took it to heart, despite never being officially introduced to the creed.

"Yeah. I'm good."

"Walid, what's wrong? You can talk to me. I remember what you did for me and Minnesota in that attic. You were brave. And I'm indebted to you for life, kid."

"What's indebted?"

"I owe you." Spacey smiled. "I just need you to tell me the truth. What's going on?"

When Walid turned around, he saw Ace standing in the doorway looking at them both.

"Leave me alone," Walid said to Spacey. Loyal above all to his twin, he stormed away, leaving him alone.

The moment he bent the corner, he was shocked to see Blaire in the hallway with The Butler who he spent most of his time with when they lived at the Petit Estate. Next to Mason, there was no other man on earth he respected more.

And The Butler, despite being creepy to most, felt the same way about the kid.

"Hey, kid!" The Butler said.

In that moment, Walid placed him on his very short Hug List and ran up to him with wide arms. The tall white man lifted him up. "Glad to see you doing good."

Blaire shook her head as she bore witness once again to the strange bond the man had with her child. Although she wasn't a Butler fan per say, she was certain of one thing. If something ever happened to her or Mason, she was sure that The Butler would protect him with his entire being.

Despite never getting their relationship, she understood it was genuine. Their bond was the only reason he still worked at the Petit Estate, since nobody else lived there. She had gotten rid of the maid, who was also a resident, a long time ago, due to never trusting her from the gate.

"You two can catch up in the living room." Blaire said, happy to see Walid in a better mood. "I'll have Morgan fix you up some snacks. And you can talk about whatever strange things men and kids talk about." She laughed, although very serious.

She was about to leave when Walid said, "Ma."

She turned around. "Yes, son."

"Thank you."

She winked and walked away.

Blaire was in her room looking for Tinsley's number when Morgan knocked on the door.

"Come in."

The house manager entered.

"Yes, Morgan?"

"How are you, Blaire?"

In that moment she smiled. "I'm fine."

"Good. Because I want you to know that I'm here for you. And Mason. If you need me."

Blaire nodded. "Means a lot."

She nodded once. "Also wanted to let you know that The Butler I believe you call him."

Blaire giggled. "Yes."

"Well he and Walid settled on cereal instead of a prepared snack." She laughed. "I couldn't talk them out of it. I'm sorry."

"Figures. They used to eat it a lot at the estate." She shook her head. "Did you make Ace lunch too?"

"Yep. He's eating in the dining room."

She nodded. "Thanks."

"One more thing, Jersey is here. With the baby. She wants to talk to you."

She frowned. "Wasn't expecting her but it's cool. Thanks again."

Five minutes later Jersey was in the lounge with Blaire speaking about a little of everything. It was mostly small conversation at first, but Blaire had an ulterior motive. She needed to know who Howard was. And she was certain, even if she lied, that she could see in her eyes if she was telling the truth.

But there was something else.

As Blaire played with Blakeslee, she couldn't get over the resemblance the child had with Minnesota and even herself.

"Why are you staring at her like that?" Jersey asked with a twinkle in her eyes.

"I don't know...she...I don't know..."

"What is it?" She was hoping she saw the resemblance and would solve her own memory loss case for herself.

"Nothing. She's cute that's all."

The air in Jersey's chest deflated. "Definitely blessed to have such a beautiful baby."

She placed her down. "Jersey, who is Howard?"

"Did you say...did you say Howard?"

"Yes."

Jersey suddenly broke down crying and Blaire immediately jumped up and sat next to her. Now she felt bad for bringing it up.

Rubbing her back softly, she said, "I'm sorry. I didn't know mentioning his name would rattle you."

Her touch alone caused her to well up with even more emotion. "No need to be sorry." She sniffled.

"Had I known—."

"It's not you it's just that, I've been so focused on other things that I...that I..." Jersey took a deep breath. "That up until this point, I hadn't mentioned my son's name."

Blaire jumped up. "Your son?"

"Yes." She sniffled and wiped her nose with the back of her hand. "He's been missing for the longest time and I'm afraid that something has happened to him. Why do you ask who he is? Did you remember something?"

Silence.

"Blaire, why did you ask?"

"What were the circumstances surrounding his going missing?"

She sighed. "Well, he, um, there was a family situation that got violent. He may have been involved and after that, he went missing. We think he is in hiding due to feeling guilty. At least we hope so."

After what Blaire saw in her dream, she was certain that Mason was responsible. And at the same time, she was not willing to hurt Jersey or him with the details.

Besides, what if she was wrong?

"Oh."

"It was just a memory, I guess. Can't remember the details."

Her eyes widened. "Try hard. Maybe there is some clue that will lead to finding him. I had an investigator on the case and—."

"Jersey, I only remembered his name. Please try not to get more worked up."

She stood up and approached her. "Are you sure?"

"Yes. If I find out something more, or have another dream, I'll let you know."

"Blaire, why didn't you ask Mason? Is it because you can't trust him? If it is, I understand."

Mason was driving down the street when his phone rang. Per usual he started to ignore it when he saw Jersey's name. Besides, things had been pretty bad with Blaire and so he had taken to the bottle harder than ever. And as a result, he was slightly over the limit.

"What now?"

"He asked me about Howard!" She yelled. "He's getting his memory back I know it!"

SCRREEEEEEEEEEECHHHHHHHHHHHH!

Mason stopped inches from slamming into the back of the car ahead of him. And so, he pulled over.

"What the fuck was that noise?" Jersey yelled.

"Never mind all that, what did you tell her?"

"I told him Howard is my son! I even lost it and started crying because it had been so long since either of us bothered trying to find him. We are awful parents."

"Anything to look like the victim."

"Aye, Mason, fuck you! Besides, what did you tell him? Because I know he asked you first."

Mason's temples throbbed. "I told her I didn't know him."

"So, you denied your own son?"

"I...I was afraid her mind would get messed up and—."

"This is what I'm talking about! You can't keep lying about who he is, Mason! He's starting to remember. Do you really wanna be on the receiving end of his energy when he gets total recall?"

"Let me handle my relationship."

"Again, I have a relationship with him too! And he's about to remember. I feel it in my soul." She said happily.

When he hung up in her face. The bitch was tripping. Concerned, he immediately called Blaire. He had to clean up what Jersey ruined by telling the truth.

As he waited on her to answer the phone, he couldn't help but relive a nagging feeling that once again he was forgetting something that would haunt him later.

What couldn't he remember?

"Blaire, I heard you spoke to my cousin." He rubbed his hand over the steering wheel.

"That's all you gotta say to me?"

The even tone of her voice made Mason shiver. Once again, she sounded like Banks. "I didn't want to tell you about Howard because it wasn't my place. It still isn't my place now."

"Why? Why the lies?"

"Because we think something happened to him. And I knew you would approach her about it, and I didn't want her to do exactly what she did. Get upset and cry."

Blaire sighed and he relished in her guilty tone. "Did you hurt that boy, Mason?"

He frowned. "Hold up, what did you dream?"

"Tell the truth for once, Mason!"

"There are a lot of things you don't know about, Blaire. And when I hold back sometimes, it's not only to protect you. It's also to protect our family. I hope you understand that now."

"Mason, this—."

"There are dark things at play. Things you won't be able to deal with alone. Let me take care of you. Okay?"

When Spacey walked into the hospital room, he was surprised to see a man he didn't recognize sitting next to Minnesota's bed as she slept. Walking deeper into the room he asked, "Who are you?"

Zercy sat the book down he was reading, stood up and attempted to shake his hand.

It wasn't accepted.

"The name's Zercy."

"That's not what I asked. Who are you? And what are you doing here?"

He cleared his throat. "I think it would be better if she told you. Our situation is a bit weird and very new." He looked at her. "But I still felt the need to be here for her."

He crossed his arms. "In what capacity exactly?"

"I don't know if I have any role here." He shrugged. "But I'll stay in whatever capacity she'll have me."

He glared. "Can you leave us alone? I want to talk to her in private."

"She just went back to sleep. Maybe you should—."

"I'm sure she wants me here." Spacey said arrogantly. "Why else would she tell them to call me?"

"Actually, I told them to reach out to you. She's been here for two days and I figured she should have somebody from the family at her side. Looked in her phone, saw the most called number and made a decision."

Spacey looked down. "So, you, so you read our text messages?"

He frowned. "No. Of course not."

Spacey nodded. "Give me ten minutes with her alone. Please."

Zercy nodded and walked out.

Strutting up to the bed, he grabbed her hand softly, clasping it into his own. "Minnesota."

Silence.

"Minnesota, open your eyes."

Her lids flipped open and she looked around. "What are you...what are you doing here? And where is Zercy?"

"He stepped out." He gripped her hand tighter as if all would be better with his presence. "Why didn't you tell me you miscarried? Why didn't you call me?"

She tried to readjust in bed but was slightly uncomfortable. "Spacey, don't—."

"I'm serious."

She sighed. "Because I knew you couldn't handle this situation. And I didn't want you worrying when I knew I was going to be okay."

"But the baby..."

"I know." She slipped her hand out of his and pulled the blanket up to her chin, as if covering her body. "The past few days have been rough. But I'm dealing with it. I don't...I think my attitude towards my baby may have been the cause of it not surviving. And I will forever feel guilty about it."

"Don't put that on your heart."

"Zercy said the same thing. But it's easier said than done."

He sat in the chair Zercy exited. "Where did you meet that guy from anyway?"

She shook her head slowly from left to right. "If I told you, you wouldn't believe me."

He crossed his leg grown man style. Ankle to knee. "I'm listening."

"Felt a bit lonely. I was on one of them dating apps. Saw his picture and liked it, I guess. But it turns out his sisters set it up because he's supposed to be moving out of town and they figured if he had a girlfriend he wouldn't leave. So they were checking me out and—."

"Stop!" He waved his hand. "So, he's a stranger?"

"I wouldn't call him that."

"Then what do you call him, Minnesota?" He laughed, although he found nothing humorous.

"You have some man going through your phone, calling folks up and you think that's sweet? If you ask me something is way off with him. And in my book, it don't add up. Plus, it's not like you have the best taste in men. Maybe you should—"

"That man has been here ever since I got here. He leaves only to wash up and change clothes. And then he comes back, sits in that chair and either reads that book..." she pointed at a blue book with ACIM on the cover. "...or he talks to me and calms my nerves. So, he may be many things, but a stranger he is not."

"Just be careful, Minnesota."

She sighed. "You have your wife. Pops has Mason. And I have nobody. So, at this point, what do I have to lose?"

CHAPTER TWENTY

Blaire stood in the front of her closet looking for the right outfit for what she had planned for the day. But after ten minutes of searching in vain, it soon became obvious that nothing fit her mood. And so, she went to Mason's walk-in closet instead.

Within minutes she decided on a pair of grey sweats and a white t-shirt. She didn't bother with her breasts prosthetics because it was all about comfort and not pleasure. Next she slipped into her Gucci flip flops and headed out the door.

When she arrived at a Strong Curls retail location which had not been opened for business as of yet, she nodded at Hercules and Aaron who were waiting outside. Grabbing an envelope off her passenger seat, she slipped out of her truck.

"It's good to see you, niece," Hercules said, surprised she was dressed down. Since her hair was pulled back into a ponytail and she wasn't wearing makeup, she looked even more like her former self.

But there were no pleasantries. She stared at him, unlocked the store and said, "Follow me."

Confused, they entered the retail shop. It was mostly empty. Just the shelves that would soon hold Strong Curl products and a register. She stood in the middle of the floor and they posted up in front of her.

"I'm going to be quick, because to be honest there isn't much to say."

They nodded.

"Your money is on pause. And I have in my hand a cease and desist order to stop you from coming to my businesses."

Aaron frowned. "I'm not understanding."

"The stipend set up by grandmother is on hold."

Hercules tried to smile to prevent from going off, but it wasn't working. As far as he knew, the stipends were set up by the lawyer and were out of Blaire's reach. "First off, you aren't authorized to—."

"Check your banking accounts. And then tell me what I'm authorized to do. I'll wait."

As they snatched the phones from their pockets, she stood patiently in total confidence. When their expressions changed from nondescript to fear, she sighed. "Like I said, your money is on pause."

"You put a freeze on my fucking banking account!" Hercules yelled. "How did you do that?"

"Why did you do that?" Aaron added. "Mother wanted us to have that money."

She stepped closer. "I did it because I don't respond well to threats. And I warned you at grandmother's funeral that I wasn't the one. You should've listened and saved yourself the trouble."

"But we...I..." Hercules was shaken and stirred. "I don't know what you're talking about."

"You have been hanging around my house. Meddling in my business. And trying to muscle me out of Strong Curls. This time you pushed too far. And because of that, you left me no choice but to snap back."

"But we haven't been meddling in anything. We have been patiently waiting for you to reconsider the—."

"No need to fucking lie, Aaron!" She roared. "I know you have been meeting secretly with Mason. I had him followed. Like I had you followed. And if you come around him or anything connected to me again, you will be cut off my payroll for life." She paused. "And let me be clear, this is not up for negotiation."

"What happens if we see a lawyer about getting our cut?"

"You'll get nothing, Aaron. And with both of your expensive tastes and the whores you patronize, you won't have enough to live, let alone fight me in court." She raised her chin. "Like I said, this is not a game. So, what are you going to do?"

The brothers stared at one another. After a brief period, Hercules cleared his throat and said, "We'll back off."

"That means staying away from Mason and my business too." She pointed at him. "And this stays between us."

They nodded.

"So, when will the money be reinstated to our accounts?" Aaron asked. The idea of having no money drove him desperately close to having a panic attack.

"Within 24 hours. Unless you think this is a game. And then it will be never." She exited without a care in the world.

When she was gone Hercules smiled and shook his head softly.

"What's so fucking funny?"

"Banks is back. Didn't you see his eyes?" He shook his head slowly. "Mason is in for a rude awakening. It's just a matter of time."

When Derrick and Nasty Natty walked out back to the deck within the Louisville Estate, Mason stood up and strutted over to the bar, barely remaining on his feet. "What you drinking, son?"

The moment he opened his mouth, Derrick realized his father had way too much already. "Pops, what's going on? You look trashed."

Mason poured three drinks of whatever was closest. Handing them each a glass, he flopped in one of the lawn chairs. Taking a sip, he said, "As you know the party is next weekend. And I need help."

"Okay, what kind of help?" Natty asked.

"First off, where is Minnesota?" He said, finally realizing he didn't give Natty a direct invite. "I didn't tell you to come here."

"Something's wrong but she didn't tell me what." She took a sip, frowned at the taste and sat the glass down. "Just said I should show up and listen in her absence."

"Did she sound sick?" Mason asked.

"No...just like she didn't wanna be bothered. She did say she was coming to the party though."

He ran a hand down his face. "Listen, I can't think about all of that right now. I just need everyone to be on point at this party. If you see someone talking to Blaire for too long, break into the conversation immediately."

"Wait, why are we doing this again?" Natty asked.

"See, this is the reason I wanted Minnesota here. I don't feel like explaining what should already be understood."

"I'm not saying she won't help. I'll tell her everything. I just, I mean, I don't get your major plan that's all." She sat in a chair.

"Yeah, Pops, I'm confused too. Don't get me wrong, I'm gonna help you do whatever you feel you gotta do. I just don't get how long you gonna draw this out."

"Exactly, because when Blaire does find out how she really lived her life, she's gonna probably feel like she can't trust you anymore." Natty shrugged. "I mean, I would be mad if somebody changed me into a man and I was a girl. Or if somebody changed me into a girl and I was a man. I mean—."

"Shut up and listen!" Mason interrupted. "I didn't wanna say anything, but before Banks' brain injury, I'm positive that he was going to admit how he felt about me."

Derrick frowned with disgust. "Wait, you liked Banks when he was dressed as a, you know, man?"

"I never saw her as a man. Never."

"Now I'm confused too. Were you or were you not attracted to Banks Wales?" Natty continued.

"Like I said, I knew her before all of that other shit. I knew her before she was ever Banks Wales. I met her as Blakeslee." He looked at his son. "And I told you this story already. She was my first girlfriend."

"I get it, I just, I don't know, now I'm starting to feel bad for Banks." Derrick was mainly grossed out. Because Banks did such a good job as trans that he saw nothing else back then.

Mason's face reddened. "What about me?"

"What about you?" Natty responded.

"I'm not talking to you!" He pointed at her. Focusing on Derrick he said, "Listen, I need to know right here and now if the both of you are going to help me. If you won't, that's fine, but tell me right now so I can get the backup I need."

"Pops, you know I'm with you. I just want you to think about the end game that's all. Because if you do this wrong, things may be worse than they ever were. And could push us back into a war."

The sky was sangria colored when Blaire walked outside on the deck overlooking the large outdoor pool. And she was surprised to see a candlelight set up with Mason wearing a short sleeve black linen shirt and matching shorts. On the table were an assortment of meat cheeses and wine, which he always pulled out when he was in the apologizing mood.

Wearing stretch pants and an oversized grey sweater, she rubbed her arms for warmth as she approached the table. "What's...what's this all about?"

He walked up to her. "I wanna apologize to you."

She frowned. "For what?"

"For everything." He grabbed her hand and led her to the lawn couch. Sitting next to her he took a deep breath. "Listen, I want to be honest with you about some things."

"You mean about Howard?"

He sat back. "Howard is Jersey's son. Like I said earlier, that part is true. And I didn't want to involve you because he went missing and nobody knows where he is." He paused. "But I'll talk to you about that later. That's not what I'm apologizing for now."

"Then what is this about?" She crossed her arms over her chest.

"You have been trying to find out more about your past and I've been holding back." He looked down. "And I know in my heart it wasn't right, but it didn't stop me."

"So, you admit that you have been trying to stop the flow of information from coming my way?"

"Yes."

Her eyes widened. "Why, Mason?"

"Because I'm scared."

"Why?"

"I'm scared about, about losing you." He paused. "Listen, things may get dark over the next few months. And I know you won't understand everything I did, even after you gain new knowledge about your past. But one thing that has always been consistent is that I love you. I have always loved you. And I want to know, I mean, do you believe me when I say that, baby?"

"Mason, this is..."

"Do you believe that I love you more than anything in the world, Blaire? I need to know right here and right now."

She looked into his eyes. It was longer than she had in a while. To be honest, lately she didn't feel the need to look at him. He wasn't about shit. And upon each new revelation and each pressure by him to be extra feminine, a place in her heart found resentment with his name.

But now it was different.

Draped in the silence, she did feel like he loved her.

And more than all, she felt like she loved him in return.

"I do believe you."

He exhaled in relief. "Good, because I want you to hold onto that more than anything. I want you to hold onto that even when shit gets bad and things *will* get bad."

"You're scaring me."

"I don't want you to be scared. I just don't want to lose you."

Her heart softened a bit. "Mason, I don't know what this is about. I can tell that there is something else underneath what you're trying to tell me. And I'm okay with not knowing for now. But I do know we are connected on a deeper level. And I'll be happy when I get my memories because I know they will be rich and full. And I know they will have you in them too."

Mason nodded although the deceit weighed on him so heavily, he couldn't hear the beauty in her words.

"I'm glad you feel that way. I wanna show you something." He got up, entered the house and returned with a beautiful silver framed photo. He handed it to her.

The moment she looked down; she covered her mouth to suppress a cry. It was a photo of Mason and Banks sitting on the stairs in front of their apartment building as kids.

Seeing them together, sealed Mason to her past in more ways than she could imagine. Although she didn't doubt knowing him as a child, up until that time all she had to go on was the moment they first reconnected at the charity ball for Strong Curls. Despite him being a stranger that day, she knew immediately they had a bond but just like with everything else lately, it was enveloped in a lie.

But the photo, well, the photo was concrete evidence that their love existed way beyond the recent moments.

"Do you like it?" Mason asked.

"I love it." She said continuing to stare at the photo.

Suddenly she stared harder.

Longer.

As if trying to summon up the past.

Her hard stare on the memoir was the main reason he didn't want to give it to her in the first place. What if looking at the photo brought everything back to mind? What if focusing on the photo reminded her about how much she hated being a girl?

What if focusing on the photo meant losing her again?

"Thank you, Mason." She held the picture closely to her chest and looked down at it again. "Thank you."

He exhaled.

For now, all was well.

For now.

It was a beautiful night as Zercy drove Minnesota to her house and pulled up in the driveway. When he parked his car, he glanced at the massive estate. The spiral driveway. The brick foundation.

The glamour of it all.

"This is your house?"

She nodded. "Yeah, it's a family home. Well, not really, our other one burned down, but this was a replacement."

"A replacement mansion? For one that burned down. Whoa." He looked at it again. "It's the biggest house I ever pulled up at."

"Long story."

He nodded. "So, is anyone in there with you?"

"No. I live alone. Spacey was staying here before but he went back to his wife. I understand. But it doesn't mean I'm not...well...never mind."

"Well are you going to be okay? Because I don't feel comfortable leaving you if you need me."

She looked down at her fingers and back at him. "Actually, do you mind coming in? For a little while."

Ten minutes later they were in the kitchen eating sandwiches and drinking homemade lemonade. Minnesota had become somewhat of a caregiver and knew her way around the kitchen.

When she got enough strength she said, "I feel like I want to tell you everything. And I never wanted to tell anybody everything in my life. I guess because I was always concerned with how people saw me."

"Whatever you want to say to me is safe."

"I was pregnant by my brother."

His jaw dropped and he tried to compose himself. "Your...your brother. The one who came to the hospital?"

"Yes."

"I don't understand."

She grabbed a napkin, wiped her mouth and explained the story as best she could. She started at the beginning and went further back and then up to the most recent event. In the end he knew about Arlyndo. He even heard tale of the

Louisville's and how she almost died by their hands. The only thing she concealed was Banks' story. And when she finished telling him her story, they were sitting on the sofa drinking tea.

And she felt at peace.

There was something to be said about letting all of your baggage go. And Minnesota dumped it out at his feet.

"Wow, I, I knew you were different but—."

"Did I scare you away?"

"Your past is not relevant to your future. So how could you scare me away?"

She put her cup down and pulled her legs closer to her body, which was tucked inside a thick grey blanket. "Who are you, Zercy? You seem so calm. And outside of my father, I never met anyone like you in my life."

He sighed. "Which part of the question do you want me to answer?"

"What do you mean?"

"Do you want to know my past? Or my present?"

She smiled. "Both."

He sat back and she could see he was uncomfortable. "When I was fourteen, I accidently killed my parents."

Her eyes widened and suddenly the mood felt dark. After all, she had him in her home. Alone. But more than that, she had him around her for days. Was he a psycho the whole time?

"What happened to them?"

"I wanted to make breakfast for them for their anniversary. And I had everything laid out. But after the pancakes were done, I didn't cut the stove off all the way. So, gas filled up in the house. It was an old house so there was already a leak. I was about to take them their meals, when I remembered I left their gifts in my father's trunk. When I went outside to get them, they had already come downstairs trying to figure out where the smell of food was coming from." He looked down.

"Oh, no." She covered her lips.

"My father smoked one cigarette every day. And when he lit that match, the house blew up. I was blown backwards, and my back was caught on the neighbor's metal fence across the street. Nicked my spine. So not only did I have to learn how to walk again, I had to grieve the loss of my parents and raise my sisters who luckily were at my aunt's house. They're triplets."

"I'm so, so sorry."

He smiled. "It's okay. I mean, it wasn't for a long time. To tell you the truth I didn't think I would make it. Held onto so much guilt that it was killing me inside. I mean, I really saw blackness during those times. And I knew I was losing my vision." He sighed. "Anyway, one day I walked into my barber's shop and he had a book on the table with the initials ACIM. And let's just say it changed a lot of things in me. Also helped me let go."

"Maybe I should read it too."

"It may not be for everybody. So, reading it is not necessary. Just know that you have to let the guilt go. You have to forgive yourself and others. And that I'm here for you."

"You don't know what that means to me. I feel so alone that I, I thought for sure you would be gone after finding out I was pregnant by my brother. But you're still here. And I—."

"I'm not a perfect man, Minnesota. At all. And the last thing I want you to do is look at me in that way or put me on a pedestal. But if you need me, I'm not going anywhere."

"I thought you were leaving town."

He shrugged. "I've been talking to God about a lot of things. And He'll use any scenario to my benefit. So, maybe my sisters meddling in my business worked out after all." He winked. "Only time will tell."

They were still on the deck when Mason stepped away from Blaire as she continued to stare at the picture he gifted her earlier that night. He reasoned he may have to *'accidently lose it'* at some point if she continued to focus too hard on the gift.

Answering the call that came through on his cell, he prepared for the worst. "What is it, Hercules?" He whispered.

"Don't worry about Strong Curls."

He frowned. "Are you threatening me? Because I warned you about threatening me when—."

"I'm not threatening you." He cleared his throat. "We decided to let the matter go."

"So, let's be clear, you want me to drop pursuing your stake in Strong Curls with Blaire?" He looked back at her and she was still staring at the photo.

"Yes. Let it go. Right away."

"Why you doing this? Because you been sweating me ever since Blaire came home. So, what brought on the change?"

"Don't look a gift horse in the mouth. Consider yourself lucky. You'll need more in the days to come."

CHAPTER TWENTY-ONE

The sun was out early as Walid and Ace sat in class inside of the Louisville Estate. There was a slight difference.

Shay had been having a tough time ever since Mason threatened her about Blaire. And although the second most important thing to her was the school she was creating, she needed a bit longer before getting ready for the day. Still, to help Celeste out, she outlined all of the assignments the night before.

But it was Celeste's turn to lead.

"Okay, boys, make sure you do all of your work and have the answers in by..." she looked at her watch. "Forty minutes."

Walid smoothed his ponytail back with the palm of his hand and slid his paper in viewing position. He really did enjoy learning. Picking up his pencil, he went to work as Ace frowned.

"How come?" Ace asked Celeste.

"How come what?"

"How come I gotta do work?" He scratched his wild curly hair and then popped the rubber band he was wearing on his wrist. "Shay not here. Why can't we play and stuff?"

Smiling, because she was actually one of his biggest fans, she said, "Ace, you still gotta do your work with your cute self." She ruffled his hair and his curls fell over his eyes again.

"But I don't feel like it."

Laughing again, for only God knew why, she said, "But you gotta do your work. I don't want Shay getting mad at me and I lose my job. Now hurry up. I'll be right back with your next assignments."

When she left Ace said, "Can you help me with my work?"

Silence.

"Walid, can you help me?"

Silence.

"Why won't you talk to me?"

Silence.

"I'll be good this time. I promise."

The thing was, he was lying, and Walid knew it too. And as a result, he had no intentions on speaking to him anytime soon. All he wanted in the moment was to finish his assignment and see his friend The Butler, who promised to come over later.

"Did you like grandmother?" Ace asked.

Silence.

"I liked grandmother." He continued. "I wish you liked her too because maybe she would still be here. To give me hugs."

For the first time in days, Walid looked over at him. Lately his brother had invoked in him a fear. A fear that he would tell his secret. A fear that he would do something really bad that would get them both into trouble. And a fear that he would hurt someone.

But Walid, a boy man of his word, would not give in to his sly threats. He decided above all that he would ignore him and so that's what he did. Regardless if he decided to snitch or not.

"You know who I don't like?" Ace continued. "Celeste."

Walid stopped writing.

He had his attention now.

"I don't like her as much as you don't like grandmother." He picked up his pencil and started writing. "That's all I'm saying." He shrugged and went about scribbling on his paper while humming.

"Okay, boys I'm going to get snacks for everyone." Celeste said returning to their desks. "I'll be back." As she ran up the steps Ace sat his pencil down. His expression seemed to be glued onto the steps that Celeste had ascended.

"I be back too."

Walid shrugged and continued to go about his work, but something didn't feel right. What was going on that had his little spirit roused?

His answer came when Celeste, while screaming, toppled down the steps fifteen minutes later. Her head hit the end table and she passed out.

A few seconds later Ace came walking down the steps behind her, with his hair pulled back in a ponytail using the rubber band on his wrist.

In that moment, he looked just like Walid.

Blaire, Mason, Shay and Derrick were all at the hospital along with Celeste's parents. Although they couldn't go inside, due to the climate with 'the virus', they were able to wait at an outdoor seating area. Things were bad. Celeste had suffered a fractured skull and had been placed in a coma to reduce the swelling of her brain.

"What exactly happened?" Celeste's mother asked, her voice laced in insinuating tones. "I mean really!"

"She fell." Blaire said plainly.

"I'm not sure about that," her father responded, looking at his wife and back at Blaire and Mason.

"Listen, if you have something to say, just say it," Mason said. "Because all of this sly shit is—."

"Who is Walid?" The father asked.

"What difference does it make?" Blaire replied.

"Before she went under, she said Walid walked up behind her, scared her and then pushed her down the steps." The mother responded. "That's why I'm asking."

"Walid?"

"That's what I said."

Slowly Blaire rose from her seat. "Listen, I appreciate everything Celeste did for our kids at the school. Because she was needed. But what you won't do is blame my sons for what happened. They are just boys and incapable of hurting anyone. Definitely not pushing a grown woman down the steps."

"Exactly," Shay responded.

"Send us the bill. We'll take care of everything." She looked down at her own family. "Let's bounce."

Mason and Shay rose.

"*Bounce?*" Shay said under her breath relishing in how much she sounded like Banks.

As they walked to the car, the whole squad was angry at the flurry of accusations hurled their way. How dare Celeste's parents imply that one of the twins shoved her down the steps.

Even though one did.

How dare they think that a Louisville or Wales was responsible for such savagery.

Even though one was.

It was Shay who put things in perspective. "Blaire, I don't think it was Walid."

"What you mean?" Mason asked instead.

"Ace been off the track lately. I think something's up with him."

Blaire and Mason walked into the twins' room. Although Ace faked like he was sleep, with the covers pulled all the way up on his head, which revealed only his curly top, Walid was sitting on the edge of the bed.

Waiting.

Concerned Mason and Blaire both pulled up chairs and sat in the middle of the room. A twin bed on the right and left of them.

"Get up, Ace," Mason said calmly.

Silence.

"Nigga, get up and stop faking!" Mason roared.

Ace hopped up and sat with his back against the headboard. It was the first time either of the twins heard Mason push off so hard.

"Oh, I didn't know we had company. Why didn't you tell me brother?" Ace said. "Hello parents!"

Mason shook his head.

"Ace, did you push Celeste down the steps?" Blaire asked.

"No, mother. I wouldn't dare."

"Then what happened?"

"How would I know?" He shrugged so hard; the tops of his shoulders touched his ears. "I like Celeste very much."

"Did you do it, Walid?" Mason asked.

Silence.

"Son, did you push her down the steps?"

"Yes." He said softly looking down.

"Why, son?" Blaire asked.

"Because."

"Because what?" Mason continued.

"Because I'm bad."

For the next twenty minutes they spent time in the twins' bedroom scolding them about their behavior. In the end they were both instructed that they were on limited punishment until they could speak to Celeste.

But the moment they left Mason said, "Walid didn't do it."

Blaire nodded. "I know." She paused. "But we still got trouble."

Blaire and Mason were in the bedroom talking about the kids with the lights dimmed low. She was concerned that something changed over the past few months that she missed with the boys.

When they were living at the Petit Estate, life seemed smooth and easy going. And now that they were reunited with family, it appeared as though things were unstable, and she wondered why.

"I have to get something to drink," Blaire said tying her robe closed. "Do you want anything?"

"A beer would be—."

"Maybe you should slow down on the drinking, Mason. We need level heads now for the boys."

He shrugged. "Just bring me water then."

She was almost to the kitchen when the doorbell rang. Walking toward it, she was surprised to see Jersey's face on the security camera screen. When she opened the door she said, "Is everything okay?"

"Blaire, I have to tell you something." Her chest rose and fell heavily as if she'd been running.

The moment she opened her mouth, Blaire could smell alcohol stemming from her breath. "Jersey, what's wrong?" She stepped outside while the door remained open. "Is this about Howard?"

"No...I mean, I, I mean, I—"

"Talk to me." Blaire said grabbing her hand softly.

"I need you to...I need you to know that..."

"It's okay, Jersey."

"I need you to know that..." Instead of finishing her sentence she pulled Blaire close and kissed her passionately. Their lips stayed connected for thirty seconds before Blaire pushed her away softly. "I'm so sorry. But I'm not into women. I—."

"Fuck is wrong with you?" Mason asked busting out the door. He yanked Jersey's arm and was preparing to punch her in the face.

"Don't do that, Mason!" Blaire said, stopping him. "She's been drinking."

"Don't come out here like it's me!" Jersey yelled at him. "You the one who's foul!"

"Yo, get the fuck up from around my house before I go off!" Mason continued.

"Mason, don't do—."

"Now!" He yelled, cutting Blaire off.

Sniffling and crying at the same time, Jersey ran to her car and pulled away from the property.

Huffing and puffing he said, "That's it! I don't want you hanging with her no more!"

"You don't get to tell me who to—."

"Oh, but I do get to tell you!" He said forcefully. "Either you choose me now, or we done altogether. But I need to know right now!" He pointed at the ground. "Because what just happened here was mad disrespectful and we both know it."

"Do you really want me to choose?"

"Yes!" His voice cracked with rage. "Are you going to be friends with her, or be in a relationship with me? Because after what just happened it can't be both."

Blaire sighed, realizing the kiss was wrong on many levels, whether she was drunk or not. "I want you."

"Good decision."

She wasn't so sure.

Mason exhaled and moved to walk back in until she grabbed his hand. "But let's be clear. That's the last ultimatum you will give me again. Ever."

Jersey sat in her car, crying hard. She thought things were going in the direction she wanted them to with being Blaire's friend, but now she realized that maybe Mason was right. Maybe some place deep in Blaire's soul, she loved Mason on a level that she never would with her.

Using her car phone, she dialed a number and waited impatiently. When the person answered, Jersey sniffled and said, "Shay, its me."

"Jersey, is everything okay?"

"I need to ask you something."

"Okay. What is it?"

"Are you okay with things being the way they are? With Blaire being with Mason." She leaned back in her seat. "And I want you to answer honestly. Because I have a feeling that when it comes to how things have been going lately, you and I are the only ones who care."

Silence.

Jersey sat up in her seat and gripped the steering wheel. "Shay, are you still there?"

"I'm here."

"What's your answer?"

"You know, I've been thinking about things too. Hard really. At first all I wanted was Banks back. That was my goal. And then when I saw how happy she appeared; I was going to let things slide until the time was right. But now things are different, Jersey."

"How?" She wiped the last tears away.

"I don't think Blaire's happy anymore. I think that somewhere in his heart, he knows this isn't his life. And he wants out but needs direction."

In that moment Jersey felt an immense sense of relief. But more than anything, she felt validated to 'ack' the fuck terrible.

"Okay, at the party I'm going to tell Banks everything."

"I think you should."

"Good. Because it's time to shake shit up!"

Walid was stressed and needed a stiff chunk of cookie dough to clear his mind. When he walked to the kitchen, he was surprised to see Morgan making lunch for the family.

"Hey there." She said happily.

He frowned. Extra smiles from strangers were not his thing.

"You getting a snack?"

"Why?"

She laughed. "Because I wanted one too."

"Well get one then."

She laughed. "Listen, I know you have been going through something with your brother."

His eyes widened. Now he was listening.

"Do you want my help, Walid?"

He nodded slowly.

She extended her hand and took him to the sofa in the living room. "Get on your knees." She demonstrated for him.

"Nah."

"Why?"

"Because I don't know you."

She laughed again. "Trust me. This will help you."

Needing relief, slowly he joined her by standing on his knees.

Place your hands together and say, "Dear God, thank you for helping me with my brother."

"Who is God?"

"Somebody who will help you when you need Him. But you gotta say the right prayer. You have to say Thank You because you know it is already done. That's called Faith."

He nodded.

"Now close your eyes and say the Prayer."

He closed his eyes but kept one on her just in case she was on some creep shit. Within a minute he was ready to mouth the words, "Dear God, Thank You for my brother."

"Thank You for helping me with my brother," she whispered.

"Thank You for helping me with my brother," he repeated. Opening his eyes, he said, "Is that it?"

"Do you believe he'll help?"

He nodded. "Yes."

"Then it's done. It's that easy."

He smiled.

River had a long day and all she wanted was to get in the shower, jump in her bed and go to sleep. Lately Mason had gone from charging her with watching over Hercules and Aaron, to keeping an eye on Jersey. Although she didn't know why, she could tell by the amount of times he called her that Jersey's whereabouts at all times was very important.

When she bopped through the apartment, in shock she walked back out, looked at the number on her door and walked inside.

It was easy to spot the confusion. The apartment looked nothing like her own.

Tinsley had decorated everything and that included ordering new furniture that was accented with tall vases stuffed with colorful faux flowers. Even the odor was different. It smelled of cinnamon and baked apples which put her at ease.

But when she saw a beautiful woman standing by the window pacing back and forth, she was stuck, especially when she began to speak.

The woman was Tinsley.

"Sure, I can set it up if you want." Tinsley said on the phone. "I mean, she does it for a living so if we make an appointment it won't be a problem at all. I got you."

River tossed her keys on the table and walked over to him. She couldn't believe that although the voice was the same, he looked nothing like Tinsley and his makeup was light and not beat hard. He was stunning.

"Okay, I'll talk to you later." Tinsley tossed the phone on the new sofa and flopped down next to it. It was so fluffy he bounced once.

"What's going on?"

"Jersey wants me to set Blaire up with my friend."

She sat next to him. "What friend?"

"The hypnotist."

River shook her head and waved the air. "Listen, I think you should stay out of it. And away from Jersey too if I'm being honest."

"Why?"

"I don't know what's going on with Mason and Jersey, but it's obviously not good." She paused. "And the last thing I need is for you to be involved while living with me."

"So, you want me to leave?" He frowned.

"I didn't say that."

"Good, because Jersey is my client and my friend."

"And Mason is my boss and my friend."

"Okay...I don't know what you want me to do, River."

Tinsley looked deflated and River immediately felt bad. "Okay, you know what, I like what we have here. The last thing I want is to be beefing with you. So how about we do this..."

"I'm listening." He said.

"We don't get involved in Jersey and Mason's thing." She continued. "And if a time comes that our wires get crossed, we'll talk to each other first."

"I like that idea."

"Good, now tell me what's going on?" She waved at her outfit.

"What you mean?"

"Where do I start?" She looked around her apartment from where she sat. "You furnished the entire place."

He laughed. "Oh, you must've forgotten. I told you the furniture would be here today. So, I set everything up before you got home."

River's mind was always in the streets, so she definitely didn't remember. "How much do I owe you?"

"River, you drop three to four hundred dollars on the counter every day for food." Tinsley laughed. "I stacked up and used the money to make things nice around here instead."

River had so much money she never spent. Essentially it meant nothing to her. "Why do all of this?"

"Because you don't have to let me stay here but you do. And I appreciate it."

River nodded. "I'm barely here. I told you it ain't nothing."

"It ain't nothing to you. But it's everything to me. So, when you come home, I thought it would be nice to have a place you're proud of."

River sighed. Outside of Mason she didn't think anybody cared about her feelings. And so, all she did was stack her money up without stopping to enjoy the fruits of the cocaine.

"Okay, so let's talk about this..." she said waving her hand in front of Tinsley. "I thought you were a bad bitch at first. You were about to get—."

"What?"

"Nothing," River said waving the air.

"Anyway, I told you I did drag." He giggled. "Well I know I can't go to my hair salon because of my ex. But I figured I could still do my Sunday drag brunches to stack up some tips." He stood up. "So how do I look?"

She shook her head. "I've seen drag but you look like a...well...woman."

He winked. "That's the magic of it all, *darling*!"

"Still..." River grew serious. "Doesn't your ex know about you doing the drag brunches? Because to me it sounds dangerous to even go there."

"I told him once before but trust me, he won't bother scanning all the drag brunch spots in the DMV area for me. To be honest I didn't get a text all day. Hopefully he's over it and I can go home soon."

"Home?" River asked with wide eyes.

"Yeah. That way you can get your place back." He got up and moved toward his bedroom, singing all the way.

River, on the other hand, was stuck.

She didn't want him to go.

CHAPTER TWENTY-TWO

Blaire had a long couple of days. Everywhere she looked it seemed as if her family was losing control. She hadn't said more than two words to Mason since he gave her the ultimatum. The twins were being mean to each other and Shay avoided her all together when she tried to talk to her.

Something was up and at the moment running Strong Curls was the only thing that brought her peace and joy. She had introduced yet another product which was showing promising results as of the latest release and focused all of her attention to the efforts.

She was sitting in the lounge inside of the Louisville Estate and was on her fifth glass of whiskey when she realized she should not have been drinking in the first place.

After all, the last two tests said she was pregnant.

As she moved toward her bedroom, she was shocked at how loopy she felt. Trying to boost her mood, she hit the bottle a little too hard and as a result, lost touch with time.

And then there was the kiss with Jersey. She couldn't seem to get it out of her mind.

Why was she thinking about her so much?

And why would Mason's cousin feel bold enough to kiss her in the first place?

When she finally made it into their room, she saw Mason asleep in bed. He was lying face down, with his back toward her. He was naked and the curves of his body looked, well, feminine.

In that moment Blaire grew aroused. Strangely enough Mason's body resembled the *Sleeping Hermaphroditus* sculpture by Gian Lorenzo. The only difference was that his head was tucked under a pillow, concealing his face.

Dropping her silk pajama pants down, she crawled in bed behind him slowly. Kissing him on his exposed neck first, she then kissed him softly along the spine of his back.

Mason, believing it was time to play, moaned at her touch. But when he tried to turn around to fuck her straight up, she pushed him back on his belly, face down, preferring to touch him in that way instead.

First, her lips trailed down the back of his neck to the crack of his ass, before going back up again. When Mason tried to turn around, again she shoved him back into the belly position. Because quite frankly, in the moment, it wasn't about him.

"Stay like this," she said, her breath wreaking of whiskey. "Just...just stay like this."

Mason was trying to obey but her touch had caused him to get rock hard. And laying on his belly put his dick in a most difficult situation. But still, he resisted the urge to control everything since she seemed to be enjoying herself so much.

And boy was she in charge.

Blinded by lust and alcohol, first she stroked his left ass cheek and then the right. Mason didn't mind a little butt massage here and there and so he relaxed a little. But she had other things in mind. And before he knew it, Blaire had slipped her fingers between the crack of his ass trying to enter his tunnel.

Mason saw black.

In total rage, he turned around and shoved her off of him. "Fuck are you doing?" He jumped up and slipped in his cotton grey sweatpants across the room. "What was that?"

"W...what?" She said, voice slurring. "We were having a good time. Why you tripping?"

"Fuck you mean having a good time? Did you just try to slip your finger into my asshole or not?"

She waved the air. "I was just—."

"I don't give a fuck what you were doing!" He pointed at her. "I don't roll like that. And whatever caused you to think that it was cool to finger me, you need to rethink it now. I ain't no bitch!"

She flopped on the bed as suddenly everything he said came to mind. "I'm sorry."

"I don't know what the fuck has gotten into you lately, and I don't care. But you better snap out of it and soon!" He stormed out of the room, slamming the door behind himself.

It was a beautiful day and Walid was running around the backyard when Ace came out. Although he was young, Walid was very strong and used running as a way to build up his strength. He had gotten the love of jogging from Blaire and as a result, he realized how much it helped him reduce his aggression although he didn't know why.

He was just about to slow down when his twin approached. "Hey, brother," Ace said catching up to him.

Walid looked over at him and was angry when he saw his hair was snatched back into a ponytail like his.

He ignored him.

"Are you still mad at me?"

Silence.

"You shouldn't be mad at your brother. It's not nice. Mother says we have to stick together. And we can't do that if you don't talk to me."

Silence.

"You being mean to me is the reason why I pushed the teacher. Maybe you should play nicer and I'll play nicer too." He shrugged.

Walid stopped running.

"Yep." Ace smiled having gotten his attention with a threat. "I pushed the teacher and I'ma do it to Shay next. And it'll be all your fault."

In that moment Walid lost it.

He grabbed his brother and tossed him to the ground. Getting on top of him, he wailed fist after fist on his stomach with all of the force he could muster. Ace tried to get up, but as noted, Walid worked out for fun, while Ace only patronized exercise if Walid was doing it.

And because of his strength, he couldn't stop him.

In that moment, for some reason, Walid thought about Morgan. He had done her stupid praying and still his brother was mean. And so, he made plans to kick her in the shin if she ever stepped to him about getting on his knees again.

When Spacey walked outside to look for Blaire and saw his brothers toppling on the lawn, he ran over to them and pried them apart. Happy to be free, Ace slithered into the house.

"Come here," Spacey said to Walid, taking him to the deck chairs. Once there, they both sat down. "Tell me what I can do. Because this thing with Ace is getting out of control."

Silence.

"I'm trying to help you, brother. But you have to talk to me."

Silence.

"Okay, how about I ask you a bunch of questions. And if I'm right, you nod."

Silence.

"Okay, are you angry with your brother?"

Silence.

"Okay, do you want me to get your mother or..." he cleared his throat. "...father involved?"

Silence.

"Did Ace hit you?"

Silence.

Spacey ran his hand back through his thick curly hair which had grown over the days. He wanted to help the little boy who in his fair opinion saved his life at Petit Mansion with cookie dough, but he didn't know what to do.

And then, he settled his mind to search for an answer. He remembered how it was to be a child, growing up at the Wales Estate. He thought about what he would have liked when Minnesota, Joey or Harris got on his nerves.

"Okay, what if I take Ace to live with me for a few months. He won't be here for Christmas but—."

Jackpot!

Suddenly Walid jumped up and wrapped his arms around him. Since everyone knew Walid had a short hug list, Spacey took the gesture very seriously.

"Thank you," Walid said, trembling.

Spacey's heart broke not only because he could tell taking him from his brother for a little while meant a lot to the young bull, but also that something obviously had him shook to the core.

"Anything for you, kid. Anything at all."

CHAPTER TWENTY-THREE

It was business as usual at the Louisville Estate. Blaire was sipping coffee and looking at Strong Curls financials when Mason walked inside. Morgan was helping the chef prepare breakfast as he walked up and grabbed a cup of coffee.

Sitting across from Blaire at the dining room table, he barely looked her way as he skimmed through the classified section of the newspaper.

"Spacey asked if Ace could stay with him for a few months." She said. "I said it would be okay to separate them until we figure out what's going on. Walid apparently is still having problems with him."

"How long did you say he could live there?" He frowned.

"Until around Christmas."

"I wish you had talked to me about it first, but I understand." He shrugged.

She sighed. "Mason, I'm sorry about last night."

He looked at Morgan and said, "Can you leave us alone?"

She nodded, turned the stove off and walked out.

"I don't know what got into me," Blaire continued. "I was drinking and the next thing I know...I don't know...I lost my mind I guess."

"You tried to put a finger up my ass."

"I know, and like I said I don't know what got into me. I feel like I'm losing my mind and I...I don't...I mean, it's driving me crazy."

"You shouldn't even have been drinking that hard. You about to have my baby."

"Everything about me is foul."

"So, what can I do, Blaire? Because the way we're going its—."

"I don't know if it's about you. I think maybe it's about me. I think, maybe I should talk to Tinsley about that hypnotist."

His eyebrows rose. "Why would you participate in that shit? The last thing you need is someone in your head right now."

"How do we know it won't work, Mason? I mean look at what happened the other night. It's obvious that something is off, and I have a feeling it has everything to do with the past. So, I need to do the hard work."

"Let me come up with an idea first," Mason said before getting up and sitting next to her. "I don't want anybody making my woman feel like something is wrong with her, simply because she acts a bit different at times."

"I tried to put my finger up your ass remember. How much—."

"Let me work some things out, Blaire. And if my plan doesn't work, then we try yours instead. Okay?" He kissed her on the lips and sat back on his side of the table to sip his coffee.

She heard his request loud and clear.

But she would have to do what was best for her. Period.

River was at home listening to smooth rap while cooking spaghetti and fresh salad. In the past she didn't want to be bothered with her apartment, but since Tinsley made it a home, she found it harder to stay away. It didn't hurt that Mason seemed not to need her as much, not even for the drug end of business. It was like everything in her life was coasting, and for the first time she saw hope. And she owed it all to her new friend.

The way she felt, who knows, maybe she would start dating again.

Her only concern of recent was that Tinsley didn't come home last night, and she figured he had met trade at brunch and got caught up. River did her best to put things into perspective because neither owed the other anything, but that didn't stop her from caring.

When the front door opened, she cut the stove off and walked into the living room. When she saw Tinsley walk inside with a battered face her heart dropped. He was out of drag and looked like he'd been through the losing end of a boxing match.

Concerned, she rushed up to him. "What happened to you?" She walked him over to the sofa.

"It's a long story." He flopped back and looked up at the ceiling. "I just wanna forget about everything and move on."

That wasn't going to work for River. Not this time. "Tinsley, talk to me. That's what I'm here for."

He shook his head and smiled. "Your voice is always so calm. How do you do that?"

"What happened, Tin?" She said more sternly.

"He came down the brunch where I worked."

River tossed herself back and ran her hand down the back of her neat French braids. "I told you not to go back there. If he couldn't find you at home, he was bound to show up."

"It wasn't like that."

"It wasn't like that?" She repeated sarcastically. "Did he find you and beat you up or not? Because now you have me confused."

Tinsley looked down. "No. I called him to the restaurant."

Her eyes widened. "Why would you do that?"

"A few of my fans bought me shots, the next thing I knew I had too many and I dialed his number. Guess you could say it was a lonely drunk dial."

"This man crashed my car, stomped you out and almost beat you to death. What part of that do you miss in your relationship because I'm confused?"

He sat up straight. "Look River, I'm not like you!"

"Fuck does that supposed to mean?"

"I'm not a lesbian. It's not as easy to find someone who wants to be with another man for life. Sometimes you have to take what you can get. And what I can get is Benji."

"I'm sorry, but did you forget that my girl left me for a nigga?"

"I didn't forget. But I...I mean...I need a man, River. I need someone to take care of me. I need to know that I will be safe. And I need to feel like somebody sees me."

"Then you shouldn't be looking at Benji because he's none of those things." She paused. "Besides, I see you."

"But it's not the same."

"Listen, having you here has done so much for me. And although we won't ever be in a relationship—."

"Yuck!"

"Exactly," River laughed. "Although we will never be in a relationship, I can still be here for you as a friend. And you haven't had somebody take care of you until you had me take care of you. Trust me." She laughed. "I will build you up, never put you down and always put your feelings first."

"River, stop."

"I'm serious. I might not be a man, but I'm loyal and I'll be here for you when you need me." She moved closer. "Just ask Mason. But you gotta leave that pistol alone, Tinsley. I'm not feeling him. At all. Okay?"

Tinsley took a deep breath. "This ain't your fight." He got up holding his stomach and walked toward the back.

"Tin!"

He stopped. "Yes."

"You don't know me if you think what I'm saying is a game. But I won't allow him to continue to hurt you."

He nodded and walked away.

The moment he left; River's phone rang. She removed it from her jean pocket and answered. "Hey, boss."

"What you doing? Find a girl yet?"

She chuckled once. "Still not looking. But I may be in the market soon."

"As much shit as I got going on over here, I don't blame you if you wait." He laughed once. "But look, I need you to keep an eye on the hairdresser for me."

River rose slowly. "Why?"

"Because I may need you to kill him."

Silence.

"River, did you hear me?"

She walked near the floor to ceiling window. "Yes, I heard you."

"Then how come it sounds like a problem? Because I know Jersey had you take him home the night of my dinner party. So you should have the address."

"I do."

"You still loyal right?"

"Always."

"Good. Wait on my next word and prove it."

Tinsley was in the shower, trying to remove blood stains from his face. He knew River was right about his situation, and at the same time he couldn't say Benji would never see him again. Because at the end of the day, no matter how violent, Benji had his heart.

When he stepped out of the shower, his phone rang with an unrecognizable number. Pulling the pink fluffy towel tighter around his body and walking to his bedroom he answered cautiously, concerned it was his ex, calling from a different number.

"H...hello."

"Tinsley?"

He breathed a sigh of relief. "Blaire, is that you?"

"Yes. How are you?"

His eyes widened. He was surprised she thought enough to ask about his feelings. After all, everyone knew Blaire was worth close to a billion and Tinsley frequently made the mistake of quantifying people in terms of financial worth.

Sitting on the edge of his bed all wide eyed he said, "I'm fine. How are you?"

"I've been better."

He nodded. "Is there anything I can do to help you?"

"Yes actually. I need the information of the hypnotist you were talking about the night of the dinner."

"Sure, anything you need!"

"But Tinsley, keep this between us. Don't even tell Jersey. Okay?"

"Yes, of course."

When the call ended, he turned around and saw River standing in the open bedroom doorway. "Who was that?"

Tinsley smiled. "Nobody."

She nodded. "Well get dressed and come out here and eat with me. It's about to rain and the view from the window is amazing."

He winked. "Be out in a few."

CHAPTER TWENTY-FOUR

It was a long day and Jersey just put Blakeslee down to sleep. She was wearing a long black lace cami nightdress with a matching robe. And the rain was pouring down so hard, she decided to get a drink and sit in the lounge to calm her nerves. Lately stormy nights reminded her of being alone, and she needed relief.

Slipping into her white furry high heel night slippers, she was almost at the lounge when the doorbell rang.

"Who is that?" She said to herself.

Walking to the door, she was surprised to see Blaire on the other side. What was more shocking was that she was wearing a grey Adidas track suit and her hair was snatched back into a tight ponytail, which was tied into a knot.

In the end she looked just like Banks.

Thunder clapped the sky.

Placing the umbrella down she said, "Sorry it's so late. But can I come inside?"

Jersey was in awe.

Was she dreaming or was Banks actually there?

"Jersey...can I come in?" She looked up at the sky and the heavy drops pounced against her face. "It's crazy out here."

"Oh, yes," she backed up, pulled the drawstrings of her robe together and allowed her entry. "I was just about to have something to drink. Please, please come inside."

"I could use one too, if you don't mind."

"I thought you were pregnant."

"I don't care."

Jersey liked those words since she didn't believe she was pregnant anyway. "Oh yes, of course. I have merlot if you like."

"I prefer whiskey these days." She winked.

Jersey rolled her eyes, realizing that whiskey was always about she and Mason. "You two love the hard stuff. But I think I have something sitting on the bar. It may have been here for a while, but you're welcome to it."

The last time whiskey was poured in that house was when Banks bought it, so Blaire would essentially be drinking her own shit.

Fifteen minutes later they were laughing and talking about the small things of life. They spoke about their favorite talk shows. They talked about the small events they experienced in their short recent time together, and they talked about life.

When Jersey got up to pour Blaire another drink, her robe fell open revealing the curves of her body and Blaire looked away. It was obvious that she was attracted to her and so Jersey allowed the robe to remain ajar.

Besides, in her mind, her body belonged to Banks anyway.

Shrugs.

Handing Blaire the glass she said, "So what brought you over here so late? Don't get me wrong, I'm glad to see you but—"

"Tired of me already?" She joked.

"Nah, you can stay all night if it was up to me." She sat next to her and sipped from her own crystal glass. "And I really, really mean that."

"Is that right? Because it sounds like you trying to get me out so..." She stood up to fake leave. "Maybe I should bounce and—."

"No, stop it, silly," she said grabbing her hand. "Sit down."

The moment their flesh connected; sparks flew.

Feeling awkward, Jersey quickly released her hold and Blaire, no longer joking, took a seat.

Clearing her throat Blaire said, "I was just fucking with you."

Jersey frowned. Blaire hardly ever cursed but Banks did. "I know."

She nodded. "Listen, I'm here because I'm lost right now, and I really need a friend. Can you be my friend?"

"Of course, Blaire. Anything you—."

"Stop." Blaire waved her hand. "When I say I need a friend I need you to understand what that means."

"I'm listening."

"I don't want any lies. I want the truth. Okay?"

Jersey nodded. "Okay."

"What kind of woman was I? Before my memory loss."

Jersey sat back in the sofa. "Why are you asking me this?"

"You got a problem with me asking?"

"Nah, but it seems like you should be asking Mason instead of—."

"Was I a lesbian or not?"

Jersey blinked a few times. "Blaire..."

"Because when I'm with Mason, and I look into his eyes, I can feel in my spirit that he means something to me. I felt it from the first time he reintroduced himself at my charity event. And yet when I'm around you something feels...I don't know..."

She placed a hand on her thigh. "Talk to me."

"Something feels original."

Jersey thought about everything. It was hard to know exactly what to say because she could send things on a different path with just a few words. And still, if she lied and Banks regained his full memory, he would hate her forever for the lies.

And at the same time, if she said he wasn't attracted to women, she could risk driving him crazy because his presence at her home in the middle of the night proved he knew that wasn't true.

And so, she decided a middle ground would be best.

"You were into women."

Her eyes widened. "I...I was?"

"Yes."

"For how long?"

"I don't know but you definitely were attracted to females."

"Does Mason know?"

Silence.

"Jersey, does Mason know?"

"No. And you can't tell him I told you either. If you do, he may be angry with me and it'll cause rifts within our family."

"So, so I was interested in women even though I was married to Mason." She stood up. "No wonder he's so frustrated with me."

She looked up at her in horror. "What do you mean?"

"Everything that has been happening with us I blamed him for not understanding. I blamed him for pressuring me into being more feminine, when the entire time I've been unfaithful emotionally! It must be tough for a man to have a lesbian wife who has disconnected in the relationship." She looked down. "I feel so bad for him now."

Jersey jumped up and grabbed her hand. This was going the wrong way. "Blaire, let me explain. You didn't do anything wrong. Mason is the one who is—."

"And how did I get here?" Blaire said mostly to herself.

She released her hand. "What do you mean?"

"Why do I know this address?" Blaire continued after realizing she drove over her house with ease. "You...you never gave it to me."

Jersey placed her hand over her heart. "Blaire, I—."

"We had sex. Didn't we?"

Silence.

"DID WE HAVE SEX OR NOT?" She yelled pointing at the floor.

Jersey dropped to her knees and started crying. "Please don't do this. Please...please don't put me in this situation. You have no idea what it means for me."

"It's simple. Stay away from me, Jersey." She glared.

Her eyes widened. "Blaire, please don't."

"You honor my wishes, and I'll keep this secret between me and you." She ran out the door.

"Blaire, don't go!" Jersey yelled running after her. "Please, don't leave me! I can't lose you again." She trudged up to the car, and right before Blaire pulled off, she grabbed at the door. "Please."

"What does that mean? You can't lose me again."

Out of breath and drenched in the pouring rain she said, "I...I..."

"Tell me now or I will never speak to you again." Time stopped as Blaire waited.

"I can't. I'm sorry."

She dropped to the wet earth, and Blaire pulled off.

Walid was on his knees praying hard, when Mason walked in his bedroom. "Your mother in here?" He paused. "Hold up, what you doing?"

"Praying."

"Praying!" He frowned. "Who taught you that shit?"

"Morgan."

He glared. "What are you praying about? You shouldn't do things you don't understand." Mason was so angry at the concept of people searching for the truth on the inside, that he was playing himself like the devil.

"I'm praying for my brother. That he will be nice when he comes back for Christmas."

Mason was so pissed he could've yelled *Bah humbug* and no one would've thought it was weird. Storming to Morgan's quarters, he yanked the door open without knocking. She tied her pink cotton robe closed.

"Mason, is everything o—."

"Who authorized you to teach my son religion?"

"No one. The boy was troubled and—."

"Look, I know you're new around here but, you are not allowed to interfere in my personal life."

"New. Sir, I have been taking care of your family for twenty something years."

He glared and slowly backed up. Was he that out of touch with reality, that he didn't know who was living in his own home? "No...no you haven't."

"Sir, are you okay?"

"You haven't been here that long!"

"I assure you that I have. I was at the other house that blew up and when you got this one, I came here with your regular cooking staff."

Feeling like he was spinning out of control, he ran to his office to investigate. Looking at the file cabinet that had been mismanaged since Jersey left him, he found check after check in her name, dating past twenty something years.

Picking up the phone, he called Jersey. "I need to—."

"Nigga, I don't have time for nothing you talking about tonight. Now she came over—."

"Shut up! And let me talk. How long has Morgan been working for me?"

"Now is not the time to—."

"How long, Jersey?" He slammed an open palm on the desk.

She sighed. "I'm busy."

"Please."

The way he begged, put her on pause. "Um, well, I remember the Wales used her first, and then when they changed the staff up, we had her. And then when Banks blew that house up you took her again. Or maybe she just went with the staff. So, I wanna say at least twenty-two years. Why?"

He flopped in his office chair. "Mason, why?"

His jaw hung open. "What...uh...nothing."

"Well I gotta go."

"Who came over?"

"What?"

"You said somebody came over. Who was it?"

"It doesn't matter. I gotta go." She ended the call, leaving him alone with his own thoughts.

CHAPTER TWENTY-FIVE

Walid was running around the kitchen helping Blaire cook dinner. Normally he would be too busy with his brother to help anyone do much of anything. But with Ace gone for the next couple of months, he was in a lighter mood. And still, when the moon hovered about the estate, he would look over at his brother's bed and feel a type of way.

It was during these moments that it was evident that he really missed his twin. And yet with him gone, he flourished, allowing the better part of his personality to shine.

"Go wash your hands and then grab the sliced pepperoni out of the refrigerator, Walid." Blaire said as she spread the dough over the pizza pan.

"Can I put it on top?" He asked happily.

She winked and he smiled.

When the pizza was decorated by the duo, she told him to get cleaned up as she walked to the room to get Mason. When she entered, he was sitting up in bed, his back against the headboard playing video games.

"Dinner's almost ready." She said leaning on the doorframe. "You joining us, right?"

"Not hungry."

"Mason, me and Walid made pizza. Join us."

He looked at her. "How is he holding up with Ace gone?"

"Better but I can tell he misses him. Sleeps in his bed sometimes instead of his own. He thinks I don't know but there's no reason for Ace's bed to be unmade since he isn't here. While his bed hasn't been touched." She sighed. "Anyway, I went to see Ace at Spacey's the other day. He seems fine. Wants to come back but I think they need a little space."

"I'm going to see about him tomorrow."

She nodded. "Mason, I, I want you to know that I'm going to try harder." She walked inside the room and sat on the edge of the bed.

"What do you mean?"

"I don't know." She shrugged. "I guess I'm realizing that what you're asking of me, to be more feminine, and to be a better wife is not wrong. Maybe I pushed back because I couldn't remember you at first. But you deserve to have a woman who will stand by your side."

And she meant it too.

After realizing that she could be unfaithful to Mason while moonlighting as a lesbian, she threw out all of her masculine clothes and took to taking care of her walk again like Gina Petit had embedded in her mind repeatedly.

"I don't want us to fight anymore. I'm finally willing to be what you need me to be. As your wife. Just, just don't give up on me."

Mason's dick stiffened.

Got her.

Finally!

Tossing the controller down he looked over at her. Could it be possible that they would have happily ever after?

"I appreciate that, Blaire. For real."

She smiled. "What God has joined together let no man tear apart, without first catching a bullet." She said before walking off.

The smile on Mason's face totally diminished like ice cream in the sun.

Besides, the saying she uttered was the mantra they repeated on the regular as friends. And he never once said it to her since she had been living as Blaire.

So how did she remember?

Mason stood in front of an exclusive and luxurious country club while paying Cheryl, the manager who was handling Blaire's birthday party that was going down the following night. She was an old white woman, who was also the owner, who preferred to be hands on with every aspect of her business. Especially when it came to collecting her coins.

"So how does everything look inside?" He asked nodding at the place where the festivities would be held. "I need perfection."

She took a deep breath and wiped the grey hair that was blowing in her face away. "It's beautiful. All things considered."

He frowned. "What does that mean? Because I don't want any games. It's my wife's night and everything has to look the part. Or—"

"I've run this country club since I bought it." She said interrupting. "Forty years to be exact. And I've seen every kind of celebration known to man. Still, to me birthdays are meant to celebrate life.

And they should be private. Not muddled with a bunch of strangers."

"You want me to take my money back?" He laughed.

She giggled. "Non-refundable remember?"

He touched her shoulder. "I'll see you tomorrow, old bird."

"Sure thing." She winked.

On the way home he thought about what the woman said. Sure, he originally wanted to throw a big party to impress Blaire. But since their relationship had been rocky, he thought about Cheryl's advice.

Why not make her birthday celebration private? While also avoiding everybody at the same time.

Calling from his car phone when he heard her voice he said, "Let's ditch the party."

She laughed. "What, Mason?"

"The birthday party!" He chuckled once. "I mean, I know it's crazy, but why have a big celebration just so people can come out, eat our food and drink our liquor? Let's get away together. And work on us."

"I thought the purpose of the party was for me to meet more of my family and friends."

"It is."

"So, let's keep the party scheduled, Mason. Don't worry. It'll be fun. I'm actually looking forward to it and I plan to relax."

"Maybe you're right."

"Look, I'm in a meeting at Strong Curls. I'll talk to you later." He paused. "By the way, Walid wants Chinese. I'll order when I get home."

"Cool."

When he hung up, he considered what she said about seeing her family and friends. The thing was, everyone who was coming to the event, with the exception of a few, were hired actors. After all, there was no way he could allow her to meet their real friends, only for them to tell her who she really was.

Now he would have to play defense.

And still, as he continued down the road, he couldn't help but think that once again he was forgetting something major.

But what?

Spacey walked into the living room and handed Mason a glass of whiskey as he spoke to Ace on the sofa.

Spacey flopped down beside them.

"...so I'm good now," Ace continued pleading his case while wiping his long curly hair out of his face. "I won't be bad anymore. I promise."

"Why were you bad to begin with, little ass nigga?" Spacey said, not buying what his little brother was selling.

"First off I'm not talking to you."

"Ayeeeeeeeee!" Mason yelled. "Watch the disrespect. He's an adult."

Ace sighed. "Spacey doesn't let me do the stuff I wanna do. I want to come home."

"And what exactly do you wanna do?" Mason asked. "Because what you better be doing are those assignments Shay sends over here."

"She actually brings them," Spacey corrected him. "She's dead serious about them getting the work done."

"I know. It's gonna break her heart when we put them back into the magnet program." Mason sighed. "But we can't have them slipping in their lessons. I need my boys to stay smart."

"I don't know, Mason. I think Shay has them on advanced levels. I know you and Pops gonna do what—."

"He's Pops!" Ace corrected him while pointing at Mason.

Mason glared at Spacey for the slip up.

"He knows I am." Mason looked at Spacey. "Don't you?"

Suddenly Ace wrapped his arms around Mason and held onto him forever. While he put on stunts and shows, Mason shook his head while Spacey rolled his eyes at his kid brother. Yet again, neither of them was buying his act.

"Let me hold onto my wallet." Mason said. "Because you laying it on thick ain't you?"

"Aye, cut out all that hugging shit and say what you want." Spacey said.

He released the hold. "I said it already. I wanna go home. So, I can play with my stuff in my own room."

"And I done already told you, you staying with me for a little while." Spacey said. "So, stop asking and get used to it. After Christmas maybe you can move back. But not before then."

Irritated with the both of them, he disappeared to the back of the house.

Mason shook his head. "I appreciate you and the wife looking out for him. He is definitely a handful."

"I can handle him."

"Where is your wife anyway?"

"The bedroom. She can't get around as much as she did before."

"Why not?"

"Picked up a little weight." He sat back. "Well, actually a lot. Thinking of getting the weight loss surgery since she can't move like she used to."

"I bet you're against that though right? Heard you love 'em big."

"I may consider it now."

"Oh really?"

"She's approaching 600 pounds for real."

"Damnn!" Mason said covering his mouth.

"Exactly."

"So how you holding up? With everything."

"What you mean?"

"We haven't really connected or spoke alone since what Howard did to you. You know, in the sauna on Wales Island."

Spacey remembered Howard raping him very well and chose to keep that time in the past. "I'm good."

"What about with you and Minnesota?"

"I said I'm good."

Mason nodded realizing he wasn't trying to go any further. "Well, let me leave. I have to—."

"You gonna tell pops after the party, right?" He interrupted. "Because we don't want this dragging out."

He rolled his eyes. "I said I was, didn't I?"

"I know what you said. Just haven't heard anything else about it that's all. Like, maybe we should have a plan. Sit him down and tell him everything as gently as possible. As a family."

"Don't worry, I'm going to tell her everything she needs to know." He rose. "I'll see you later." He placed a heavy hand on his shoulder. "And thanks for looking after your brother."

"Mason..."

He stopped walking. "Yeah?"

"I'm not going to let this go on forever. Just so you know."

CHAPTER TWENTY-SIX

Holding his cell phone, Spacey walked out on his deck and sat down, while overlooking his yard. It wasn't as big as the Wales or Louisville estates, but it was something to be proud of for sure.

Once comfortable, he called Minnesota's cell. But instead of getting her, a man answered. With a frown on his face he asked, "Who is this?"

"Zercy. You want Minnie?"

He frowned harder. "If I were you, I wouldn't let her hear you calling her that. It rubs her the wrong way."

"She was the one who gave me her nickname."

His eyes widened as he experienced extreme annoyance. "Nigga, put my sister on."

As he waited, he could hear Minnesota giggling as she came to the phone. "Hello."

"So, you got this nigga answering your phone now?"

She settled down. "Spacey, is something wrong?"

"Nah."

"Then why you sound like that?"

"What's up with you and this dude, Minnesota? You met him on an app, got him answering your phone and you probably at the house ain't you? Alone with a stranger."

"Yeah, so what."

"So, you have to be careful, Minnesota. You don't know this nigga and it's easy to take advantage of you."

"Spacey, I don't wanna argue with you. But this is my life and I'm going to live it as I please. Period. Now is that the reason you called? Because if it is, I'm done talking."

Spacey pushed up from the lawn chair and paced in place. When Ace came out and hugged his leg, he hoisted him up by the back of the shirt and tossed him back inside, closing the sliding glass door afterwards. He could've sworn Ace threw up the 'fuck you' finger as he walked away, but he couldn't be sure.

"Spacey!" Minnesota yelled. "Are you there?"

"Yeah, uh, that's not the only reason I called. I've been thinking about how I handled things between us. And I want you to know that I'm sorry."

"Spacey, I'm over that now. You can let it go. I have."

"Why do I feel like you're lying?"

"I wish I knew. But I have moved on. I'm actually happy now."

Happy?

Fuck she have to be happy for?

He left her ass.

He sat back down feeling slightly embarrassed. "So how you think this party is going to go down? Because I have all intentions on letting pops know what the deal is after it's all said and done."

"I think you should stay out of it, Spacey."

Finally, he had some emotion out of her. "You can't possibly still be cool with what Mason is doing."

"It's not that I'm cool with it. I happen to believe we should stay like we are born to be. And pops was born a woman."

"And pops has been a man all his life too. So how do you know he wasn't born to be a man?"

"Spacey, leave it alone, chile! Bye!"

When Minnesota ended the call, she nestled up into the corner of her sofa where Zercy was waiting.

"What's wrong?" He asked touching her leg.

"What happened on the show?" She cleared her throat. "What I miss?"

"Minnie."

She sighed and looked down. "I have to tell you something else, Zercy. About my family again."

And so, she unfolded everything additional she hadn't told him. Over the days he had become her catch all for everything she wanted to get off her heart. What made it easy was that he appeared to suspend all need to judge, and that made her trust him even more.

"So, your mother was actually living her life as a trans male and now he is living female because his best friend was always in love with him and took advantage of his memory loss."

She nodded. "What do you think about me now?"

"It's heavy."

"Zercy..."

"I don't know what you want me to say. I know we create our own experiences and then when they blow up in our faces, we blame everybody else. But

Mason is out of his league on this. Because you can't change what's in a person's heart. So that if your mother chooses to be male, she will find a way to be male again, and anybody who stood in the way of that will probably wish they never had."

River and Tinsley were in the living room singing *Can You Stand The Rain* by New Edition. Lately they took to playing oldies but goodies loud throughout the luxury apartment while dancing, and when they were together time seemed to fly by. It was obvious that the two had grown thick as thieves and their bond was only solidified by their desire to have a peaceful home above all else.

They were doing a good job too. Choosing to watch only funny movies, cartoons and eat breakfast food at night.

They lived in peace.

And when it came to a serene environment they ruled.

Tinsley turned the music down. "We going to be late for this party if we don't hurry up."

"I was thinking the same thing." River said flopping on the sofa next to their cell phones.

"I wanna ask you something." He sat next to her with a serious look on his face.

"Listening..."

"Do you think I should dress in drag for the party?"

Her eyebrows rose. "I think you should if you want."

"But do you think anybody would get upset?"

"Jersey wants you there. And I want you there. So, if you want to go, you should dress in what's most comfortable for you. If anybody got a problem with it, let them sort it out."

He jumped up, kissed her on the cheek and ran toward the back. "Wait until you see my dress!" He yelled from his room. "You'll love it!"

River shook her head and laughed.

And suddenly the feeling hit her hard. For the first time in a long time she was really happy. She and Tinsley vibed because River was laid back and Tinsley was hype about the smallest of things. And unlike their other friends, which were few and far between, they weren't trying to push one another to change.

She was just about to get dressed when she saw a text message come through on Tinsley's phone. Looking in the direction he ran, when she focused back on the cell, she saw it was a message from Benji.

It simply read: **I MISS U**

Annoyed, River jumped up with his phone in hand and paced the floor. The last thing she needed was him getting beaten again by a man who claimed to love him.

What was worse was that Tinsley fell for the trap every time. In the short period that he had been living with her, he had been beaten a total of four times. And she was tired. Tired of wiping his tears away, cleaning his wounds and building him back up, only for Benji to tear him down again.

And so, disguised as Tinsley she responded: MEET ME AT MY PLACE.

Benji: OKAY.

Feeling anxious, she erased the message and dropped it back on the couch, to hide having picked it up in the first place. Grabbing her keys, she yelled, "Aye, Tin, I'll be back in a little while!"

"Okay! Hurry back!" He yelled from the back of the apartment. "Cinderella needs her prince!"

She ran out the door.

Shay and Derrick whose relationship had been rocky for months, spent their time getting ready for the party in the same bedroom. When Derrick walked by and Shay purposely stomped his toe, he grabbed her by the shoulders and slammed her on the bed. She bounced twice and hiccupped.

"Fuck is wrong with you?" She yelled.

He flopped next to her. "I'm sick of the dumb shit. You not telling me nothing. What's up, Shay?"

"You mean outside of the fact that your father threatened me, and you didn't say anything to him?"

"What exactly did you want me to say?"

"Outside of, *'excuse me, but don't threaten my FUCKING WIFE?'*"

"Shay!"

"I'm serious! You are singlehandedly allowing him to get away with madness around here, and you don't care."

"Again, Banks was born a woman. So, what harm can come from my father helping him live the right way?"

"Live the right way. By giving him dick?"

"Yes!" He jumped up and tossed his arms in the air. "Let's be clear, I was never with Banks roaming around as a man in the first place. I always, always had a problem with it. I just remained quiet because he was the boss. But when it comes to—."

"You lying! You bought into him being a man just like everybody else!"

"I wasn't feeling it."

"So, because you not feeling it, it means it's okay to take him away from who he wants to be?"

"Shay!"

"Fuck that! Answer the question."

"I won't."

"Why?"

"Because you going to get mad."

"I want to know, Derrick!"

"Okay, Banks being a man is weird as fuck to me."

"If you lose me, it'll probably be because of this."

"Shay, shut up."

"And I also want to go on record saying one thing. When my father realizes what has been going on, everybody who participated in the lie is going to pay."

"Don't threaten me."

"I'm not threatening you. I'm stating the facts."

"Facts or not, you better not be the one who says anything to him. Or I'ma flatten them lips."

"So, are you threatening me now?" She asked.

"I said what I said." He walked toward the door. "Now hurry up and get dressed. We got some place to be remember?"

When he left, she grabbed her phone and texted Jersey.

Shay: Are we still going to tell my father tonight?

While she waited on the response, she did her makeup. But fifteen minutes later she still hadn't received a reply.

Shay: Don't back out on me now Jersey. Please!

CHAPTER TWENTY-SEVEN

I t was party time...

When Mason pulled up at the Louisville mansion in a royal blue Vision Mercedes Maybach Cabriolet, he had a smile on his face. He knew he would shut shit down as he cruised down the highway in the not for sale dream car, and those were his exact intentions. The top was dropped, and he looked as slick as a wet recently paved black road.

He also allowed his five o'clock shadow to make an appearance which complimented the black designer slacks he donned that waved every time the wind hit him ever so gently. Instead of being on his all black bullshit per usual, he chose to accent his fit with a red shirt that was slightly unbuttoned at the top, exposing a little hair on his chest.

The man looked good enough to eat.

Real talk.

When the door to the Lou Estate opened his jaw hit the floor when he saw Blaire.

Breathtaking.

She was wearing a long sleeve tight red dress and her hair was blow dried straight which caused it to run down her back. Because she was wearing her prosthetics, her physique took on a mad feminine stance. And her makeup was as light as a baby's breath, but still enhanced her beauty.

In a word she was stunning.

Mason was in awe and realized in the moment that the risk of his secret coming out tonight was worth it, just to see her dress so beautifully. But the moment she took her first step he could also tell that she was drunk.

Concerned, Mason ran up to her and helped her to the car.

"Are you okay?"

"Yes, I, I just had a little too much to drink."

"You forgot you pregnant?"

"Mason, tonight is my night."

"I'm not getting mad. Just wanna know why you started without me."

"Something like that."

Once she was tucked in the passenger's seat, he rushed to the driver's seat. "Why do you look beautiful and sad at the same time?" Mason's breath rose heavy in his chest as he waited for his answer.

Please don't leave me. Please don't leave me. Please don't leave me.

She smiled. "This car is beautiful."

"I was able to cop this from the dealer. It has to go back because it's a concept car, but I wanted it for you tonight. I hope you like it."

She nodded and looked around. "I love it."

"Blaire..." he touched her hand. "Baby, what's wrong?"

"Mason, can I trust you?"

Those words rang heavier than usual. She asked him about trust many, many times before, but this felt different.

"Of course. Of course, you can."

She looked down at herself, as if she were seeing her dress for the first time. "Why do I feel like a fraud in this dress?"

Drunk and high out of his mind, Benji took the last pull off of his blunt and tossed it in the bushes in front of Tinsley's apartment building.

"Hey, why would you do that?" An elderly woman asked who was exiting the property.

"Bitch, fuck you and mind your own business." He walked through the door.

The moment he used his key to enter Tinsley's crib, he was shocked that another guest greeted him instead. River was posted up in the corner, in the green recliner. She appeared so comfortable, it almost looked as if it were her crib.

"Who are you?" He asked stumbling a little. "And where's Tinsley?"

"You don't remember me?"

"Nigga, where is Tinsley?" He looked around from where he stood.

"It doesn't matter." She sat up.

He laughed. "Oh yeah."

She removed the gun that was tucked on the side of her leg and walked up to him. Suddenly all arrogance dropped to the seat of his balls where it belonged. "Yeah." She repeated.

He tried to run but before he could escape River shot him in the calf. His head bumped into the end table as he dropped to the floor. Rolling over on his back, he reached back at his leg and cried out in pain.

"Shut up," she said calmly.

"It fucking hurts!" He yelled louder.

The sound of his agony arrested her soul and so she got louder. "Shut up! Just...just shut up!"

"Why are you doing this?" He cried. "I didn't do anything to you. I don't even know you."

His answer was part true. And at the same time, he did crash his car into hers, so it wasn't one hundred percent factual either. "So, so you like beating up on people who don't want you? You...you like hurting people who smaller than you?"

"What?! No!"

"You're probably the type that beats up on him and then get off don't you? You're some sick ass pervert who likes to see people in pain just so you can bust a nut? Is that your thing?"

As Benji looked up at her, he grew horrified. Her eyes appeared to be darker, and he could tell saying the wrong thing could surely send him to his grave. "Listen, I don't know what's going on with you, but what you're describing is so far away from who I am it's not even funny. Yes, I hit your car, but I did not beat up Tinsley after the first time. And if he told you that he's lying. Whatever is going to happen here will happen. But I will die on that truth."

What he was saying didn't make sense.

River walked away and paced the floor. The hand that held the gun rested on top of her head while the other hand hung on her hip. There was so much to think about.

First off, she had no business bothering this man. He wasn't her problem. And at the same time, in her opinion he was trouble for Tinsley and the world would be better off without him.

"You don't want to do this," he pleaded. "I...I can tell you're a good person. If you let me go you will never see me again."

"I don't like who he is when you're around."

"So that's your only reason for doing this? Because of Tinsley?"

She stopped walking and aimed.

"Please don't kill me. I'm begging you."

"You should've left him alone."

"Please d—." She shot him again in the middle of the forehead. After she watched the life drain from his body, she ran to the kitchen sink and vomited down the drain.

After calming Blaire down by playing smooth R&B, they arrived at the venue. Mason was in awe because the view exceeded his expectations. The scenery outside resembled an enchanting forest. All of the trees were lit with white lighting that twinkled softly. As he parked the car in the front, before handing his keys to the valet driver he said, "You dent it, lose it or scratch it you die in it."

He swallowed and said, "Yes, sir." He had to adjust his dick the car was so fucking sexy.

Mason helped Blaire out.

The moment they walked inside, the room, which was outfitted like a winter wonderland, took her breath away. There were white trees everywhere and the walls were covered in white curtains that were backlit with soft blue lights. Each table was outfitted with candles and expensive antique dinnerware which oozed romance.

She was so in awe, that she didn't see the people until they stepped out of their corners and yelled, "Happy Birthday!"

With that, strangers who claimed to know her, all hired actors of course, one by one stepped up and shook her hand. She was overwhelmed hearing them recant the scripts they were given on how they met her in various times and places.

And when Mason saw her appear a little overburdened, he walked her to their table that was set up in her honor. It was designed in the Last Supper style.

"Are you okay?" He asked, taking his seat next to her as soft rap music lit up the background. "I mean, do you like it?" He looked around.

"Yes, I...I mean..." She looked up once and then down again.

"Don't worry about all these people," he said loud enough to be heard over the background. "None of them matter. Say the word and I'll throw them out on their asses."

"No, it's not like that."

"Then tell me what you need, Blaire. I'll do anything to make you love me. To make you see me." He spoke like a man who knew the hourglass had run thin of sand.

"I just wish I knew all of these people. Having them come up and tell me stories about the past just messed me up. I'll be fine." She squeezed his hand. "I've been praying on it."

He glared. "Fuck is up with all this praying shit?"

She frowned. "What's that supposed to mean?"

"First Walid and now you." He shook his head. "It's crazy. Are ya'll trying to get away from me or something?"

Instead of going off she allowed the guilt of her possibly being a lesbian to push her in line. "I'm sorry, Mason. I know you put so much into the night and I wish I could be a little more appreciative."

He touched her chin and turned it in his direction. "Listen, everything will be fine. And you already know how I feel about things. If at any point you aren't enjoying yourself, we can bounce."

"Are you sure?"

"Yes. I—." Mason's heart dropped into his left ass cheek when he saw who appeared to be Preach standing across the room staring in their direction.

And boy was there history.

When Banks had his botched-up brain surgery and was taken from Jersey's house by Gina Petit without Mason's knowledge, it was Preach who told Mason that Banks was dead and buried. Mason spent years believing that was the case until while looking for his twins, he found the three of them instead.

While Preach, just disappeared, never to be seen again until now.

So, what was he doing there? Posted up at a party he wasn't invited to, wearing all white with his hands tucked in his pockets. And staring their way.

"What is it?" Blaire asked. "You look like you seen a ghost."

He jumped up, bumping the table in the process. "Nothing. The...the...the...the...fam...the fam..."

"Mason, what's wrong? Why you stuttering?"

"The rest of the family should be here in a minute. I'll be back when I can."

She grabbed his hand before he made a clean escape. "Mason, are you sure you're okay? Are you sure there's nothing that you want to tell me?"

He bent down and kissed her lips. "I'm fine. Don't worry about me. Tonight, it's all about you."

Those words were facts.

River was in the shower with her forehead penned against the wall. She couldn't believe she killed a man without authorization from Mason. And more than anything, she wasn't entirely sure why she pulled the trigger.

She murdered a civilian.

This was not who she was. At her core she was a calm person. A loving person and a gentle soul. But during office hours, or when she worked for Mason she was something different. The thing was, she was not at work when she became the executioner.

Unfortunately for Benji, built up aggression from River losing her girl, losing the life she thought they would share and losing her mind, made him an easy target of which she took full advantage.

"River, we're going to be late!" Tinsley yelled cheerfully outside of the bathroom's closed door. His mood. The exact opposite of hers. "Hurry up! I feel good for the first time in a long time! I wanna have fun!"

River raised her head. "I...I know."

"Then hurry up!" He giggled. "And where did all this dirt come from? It's everywhere."

River looked down at the dirt granules that covered the drain. The dirt was relatives of the earth that covered Benji's body that was tucked deep in the ground.

"I'll be out in a second."

"Well hurry up because I feel like singing!" Tinsley yelled.

Suddenly the music blasted, and Tinsley happily ran up to the door again. It was *New Edition's*, *'Can You Stand The Rain'*. "It's our song! Come sing with me!"

River couldn't help but force out a laugh. Tinsley's energy was contagious, and it made her feel like she had made the right choice after all. Despite knowing in her heart that she was wrong.

An hour and two drinks later she was dressed and ready to go.

River was definitely fine as fuck in the moment. Wearing black slacks and a black button-down shirt embezzled with paisley patterns with the sleeves rolled up to reveal a gold watch on one wrist, and a leather cuff bracelet on the other, she looked like a snack.

But it was Tinsley who stopped the show.

After hearing it was a winter wonderland theme, in full drag, with a lightly beat face, he chose to wear a medium length spaghetti strapped white dress that flowed when he walked and rhinestone heels. The wig of the evening was circa Beyonce style, and it cascaded down his back in waves.

He did not look like Tinsley.

He looked like a beautiful woman.

"Wow, you are unrecognizable!" River said as her eyes rolled from his feet to the top of his head.

"And you a snack." She grabbed the hem of her shirt. "Between the two of us we're definitely getting laid tonight."

"I'm good on that," River winked. "But I want to see you have fun." She held out her arm. "Any man would be lucky to have you."

"You think so?" He looped his arm through hers.

"I know so, Tin. Trust me. The man who deserves you will come along. Just be patient."

He smiled and wiped the hair out of his face. "Ready?"

"Couldn't be readier. Let's roll."

Tinsley was about to walk out the door when he realized he didn't have his phone. Unlooping his arm, he ran to the sofa. "I been so busy I haven't even looked at my phone all night. Time flies when we are together." He grabbed it off the couch from where he last left it.

"Oh yeah."

Hoping he wouldn't catch on to her deceit, River shuffled in place, knowing full well that she used it to commit the greatest sin earlier in the night. And so, she waited to be found out.

"Let's go, Tin."

"One minute." He responded as he scrolled through his phone.

Clearing her throat, River asked, "Everything cool?"

He slowly raised his head and smiled. "Couldn't be better." Dropping his phone into the white caviar quilted medium Chanel Boy bag he was carrying; he looped his arm through River's again. "Let's go have a little fun. We deserve it."

"Now you talking."

The party was on full fledge spectacular as Jersey pulled up looking drop dead gorgeous. She was wearing a long red chiffon style dress, and with a split all the way up the front, it revealed every cut of her toned leg. She was as sexy as a detailed car and as drunk as a baby on sugar.

In other words, for Mason, she was trouble.

The moment Blaire saw her face, her jaw dropped. And Jersey was gifted the opportunity to catch the gaze too.

Got 'em. She thought to herself.

Spotting the Last Supper Table set up, Jersey waltzed in her direction and tried to sit next to Blaire, until River stopped her by pulling out the chair. Jersey almost hit the floor.

Looking her up and down Jersey smiled. "Even though you could've killed me just now I must admit. You fine as fuck."

River couldn't be bothered to accept the compliment. "Mason said you can't sit over here." She pointed over the wig she was wearing and clear across to the other side of the room.

Jersey was preparing to do what she came to do, *'ack'* a fool, when Minnesota and Zercy walked inside.

"Everything cool?" Minnesota asked.

"First off, I don't have to ask for permission to sit next to my family," Jersey said pointing at Blaire as if she were a fixture. "I mean really, who the fuck are you anyway? It seems to me that Mason loves having him something yellow, dominate and mean at his side at all times."

Jersey looked down at Blaire although River didn't understand the reference. Blaire didn't either for that matter.

"It don't matter who I am. You can't sit over here. Period."

"It matters if you're trying to get me to do something I don't want to do," Jersey said.

"What's going on exactly?" Blaire asked standing up.

She was going to leave the matter alone, since she believed she had been in a secret lesbian relationship with Jersey, but since things were heating up, she felt she had to step in.

"This person is trying to prevent me from sharing your party," Jersey continued swaying and talking loudly. With each syllable she was throwing her sex appeal out of the window. "And I'm not having it. Not tonight. Now we may have had our problems but we still family!"

"Is everything okay?" Minnesota continued while standing next to her date. She was wearing a modest black dress. Zercy, by her side who sported a black suit.

"No, no, everything is not okay!" Jersey yelled. "I'm sick of this shit! I'm sick of having my life rearranged and nobody giving a fuck. What about me?" She stabbed herself in the center of her chest with her thumb. "What about what Jersey wants? Huh?"

"Please go sit the fuck down," River said pointing over her head again.

"What does that mean, Jersey?" Blaire asked Jersey.

"Now is not the time," Minnesota said gripping Jersey's hand. "Please don't do it like this."

Jersey looked at Minnesota, Zercy, River, Blaire and now Spacey and Shay who just entered the party. They were all standing behind the table, looking dazed and confused. Each wondering who would pull the tattle tale trigger.

Taking a deep breath, Jersey asked, "Where am I supposed to be sitting?"

"Over there," River pointed over her head again.

"Nah, this table big enough for me. I'm sitting here." Everyone took their positions, despite River trying to keep Mason's set up. She would've unleashed and got violent, but she had already killed a man that evening. Also she didn't want to disrespect Mason's family.

At least no one was sitting directly to the left or right of Blaire.

When everyone was seated, River took her position next to Tinsley, who was so unrecognizable that not even Jersey knew it was him. And because Jersey was embarrassing above all else, Tinsley was fine being incognito.

"Is everything okay?" Tinsley whispered to River.

"Nah." She looked to the left and right at the Lou and Wales family members. She watched Shay who walked over to Jersey, stooped down and started what looked like a sneaky ass conversation. "I got a feeling shit is about to get wet in here."

"Sit down, Shay!" Derrick yelled.

"Nigga, fuck you! Because secrets are coming out tonight! Believe that!"

Unable to wait until later, Spacey walked up behind Minnesota who was sitting at the table and touched her arm. Nodding toward the wall he said, "Hey, can we talk in private?"

"Damn, nigga, you slide in wearing a white suit and then act like you don't see nobody else?" Shay said standing up in front of him.

"I told you not to have that third lemon drop," Derrick told her. "But you wouldn't listen."

"Am I talking to you though?" She said rolling her eyes at her husband.

"You gonna make me fuck you up in here." Derrick nodded in all seriousness. "I promise. And not a Wales in the building will be able to pull me off of you."

"Whatever, man," She sat down.

"Minnesota, please," Spacey said ignoring them both. "Can we talk in private?"

She looked at Zercy and said, "I'll only be five minutes."

"Take all the time you need."

Scooting back in her chair she walked over to the wall, "What do you want?"

"I made a mistake."

She frowned. "Made a mistake about what?"

"Us."

"Spacey, stop tripping."

"I'm serious. I let us growing up together get in my head, and now I'm realizing what I want. It's you."

"Spacey, please."

"Just hear me out," he sighed. "I...I mean...we aren't blood related, Minnesota. There's nothing to stop us from being together if that's what you want. If that's what *we* want?"

"What if it's not what I want though?" She shrugged.

"So, what changed all of a sudden?" He pointed at Zercy at the table. "His green ass? Because I'm five seconds from going off if—."

"Spacey, we may not be related but we are both still Wales'. And the one thing I know about Wales' is that we never appreciate what we have until it's gone."

"What does that mean?"

"You don't want me because you want me. You want me because I don't want you." She touched his face and rejoined her date.

Just then, in an effort to seize the moment, Jersey flopped next to Blaire and River rushed up behind her, lifted her up like a bride going over the threshold, and tossed her down in her seat.

Because if Mason made one thing clear, it was that he didn't want Jersey anywhere near Blaire.

Seeing the foul against his mother, Derrick stormed in her direction. "My nigga, I know you didn't just toss down my moms."

"Did you see her drop?" River asked.

"I did."

"Then I guess it was me." Derrick stole her in the face and a fight erupted.

CHAPTER TWENTY-EIGHT

Mason and his men had cornered Preach in the kitchen of the venue. Every chef was told to evacuate.

"Fuck are you doing here, man?" Mason yelled as his men surrounded Preach. He couldn't believe he had the audacity to show up to the event, when he hadn't seen him in years. "Are you crazy or high?"

Preach raised his head. "I needed to see if it was true."

"If what was true?"

"If you used Banks' memory loss to your advantage."

"Nigga, whatever."

"What are you doing to Banks, man?" He said passionately, placing a hand over his heart. "He's your fucking friend! And you use his memory loss to...to...fuck him."

"Don't be stupid! It ain't about sex."

"Then explain it to me!" He yelled. "Help me understand. Because when I heard what was happening, everything in my spirit told me to stay away. To stay in hiding. And to not give up my location. But I would rather die than know you are forcing him to live a life for your benefit. A life that he never would've chosen for himself."

Mason felt gut punched by his words.

"You don't know the life we have together now. You don't know what we mean to each other now. You aren't around us twenty-four seven and—."

"Banks is trans! He made a decision to live as a trans man. Now I don't know what's involved in loving who you want to love, but I know that living his life male was what he wanted before the surgery. Now if he loved you or not, is not my department. But if you cared about him, like you claim to care right now, you should've accepted him physically as Banks. And not change him. I mean, what are you going to do when he remembers? And he will remember. Trust me."

Mason lowered his brow sensing the threat. "You should've stayed away."

"And you should've honored your friend more than you're doing right now. So that makes two of us."

"Aye, Boss, shit is getting crazy right now," River said running into the kitchen. Her lip was busted, and her eye looked on the swollen side.

"Me and your son just got into a fight and I think some shit's about to—."

The interruption allowed Preach to run out the back door and into the night.

"Catch that nigga!" Mason directed his men. "Don't let him get away!"

Mason and River ran back to the party scene only to see that everyone was gone. But it was Blaire's disappearance that startled him the most. The only one at the table was Tinsley dressed in drag, who looked like a beautiful woman.

They were both standing next to him as River tried to explain everything that occurred.

"Fuck!" Mason said looking at the strangers who were dancing about the party on the dance floor, totally oblivious to the fact that the Lou's and the Wales were going through possibly their biggest controversy yet.

"Sorry, she must've left when I came looking for you." River said. "And my bad about your son too."

"He built tough. Don't worry about that part."
He looked her over with a concerned eye. "Are you okay?" He put a hand on her shoulder.

"I'm good."

He nodded, removed his hand and observed the room from where he stood. Mason could sense his life about to crash down around him. Taking a deep breath, he said, "Listen, I have to find Preach." He moved to leave but returned to River. "And that hairdresser, what's his name?"

"Tinsley."

"Kill him. I don't need any more fuck ups."

River frowned. "W...why kill the hairdresser?"

He glared. "Because I don't need any loose ends."

River was confused by it all. "So, Blaire getting her memory back is a loose end?"

Mason was incensed. "You asking too many questions. Whatever happened to say less?"

"But I—."

"JUST DO WHAT THE FUCK I SAID!" He yelled so loudly, everyone looked over at them. "Okay?"

"Yes."

Taking a deep breath, Mason said, "Look, you're like a daughter to me. But it is important that you remain loyal above all else. Never question me again." He ran off.

When River looked down, Tinsley was shaking so hard, he peed in his pretty white dress. Quickly he pushed back his chair and ran out the door as River gave chase.

Grabbing his hand, she yanked him toward the side of the building. "Calm down, Tin."

"Calm down!" He repeated with wild eyes. "Did you say calm down? I mean what is going on? Why...why does he want to kill me?"

"I don't know."

"Are you going to...are you going to kill me?" He was so hysterical he could hardly keep still. "Because I don't wanna die. Please. I don't wanna—."

River snaked her hand behind the back of his head and placed her lips against his ear. With all the passion in the world she said, "I'm not going to kill you. I don't care what he says."

"I'm scared." He cried.

She looked into his eyes. "Believe me. Trust me. Okay?"

He nodded.

"Now take the car and go to our apartment. I'll be there when I can."

Tinsley kicked off his shoes and ran away.

CHAPTER TWENTY-NINE

The party was a complete and utter disaster. And last night, while everyone called his cell phone like journalists reporting a riot, Mason ignored their calls, Sending each of them to voicemail. And so, as he lie in bed, alone, he came to the realization that Blaire did not return to him the night before.

She didn't even call home.

A witness to her silence, he was certain he lost her forever.

As he sat on the edge of the bed, with the curtains open revealing the anxious sun, he was angry that it didn't provide him with the light he needed to see clearly. He had fucked up and since Mason Louisville only did things big, he knew he didn't fuck up a little.

He fucked up greatly.

When he trudged into the kitchen to grab a cup of coffee, he wasn't surprised to see Derrick and Shay eating a small breakfast yelling at each other per usual.

At least that part was normal.

Shaking his head, he walked over to the pot and sighed. "Go ahead. Tell me what happened last night?"

"So now you want us to tell you?" Shay said. "You wouldn't even answer the phone or door last night. Like you didn't start all this bullshit."

He shook his head. "You know, I don't condone beating women but if you ever get the urge, I'm okay with it, Derrick."

Derrick cracked his knuckles and grinned at Shay.

"I wish he would." Shay said reaching for a butter knife.

"What happened at the fucking party last night?" Mason asked.

Derrick ran his hand down his face. "Well, ma made a scene and the dom chick started arguing with her about sitting next to Blaire and—"

"Her name is River. And she's loyal. So that makes her family."

Derrick waved the air. "Whatever her name is, she got out of line when she tossed ma like trash. Anyway, Banks got upset and left. Everybody chased him but they couldn't catch him, and he got away in some car. With everything turning to shit, instead of going back to the party everybody just went home."

Mason pulled out a chair, placed his coffee cup on the table and flopped down. "This doesn't feel good. Something is—."

"Where everybody at?" Minnesota and Spacey asked walking into the kitchen. They were dressed down in very similar track suits and looked frazzled.

Mason frowned. "What you talking about?"

"Got a text to be here in an hour." Minnesota said.

"I thought we were late." Spacey responded looking at his watch.

"Who texted you?" Mason asked.

"Blaire," Minnesota said in a whisper.

Trouble was on the way for real.

As they waited with small talk around the table, Mason zoned out. All he could hear was the thump of his heart as his blood coursed speedily through his veins. He didn't know what was going to happen, but he was sure life as he knew it over the months had changed.

And then it happened.

Ten minutes later, Joey walked inside the house followed by Blaire and Preach. They all looked serious like business. And Blaire was dressed down. Sweatpants. A plain white t-shirt with a fold line down the middle which indicated it was fresh out the package. And her hair pulled back in a tight ponytail, Walid Wales style.

They looked sinister and Mason moved to grab his gun under the table, but Derrick stopped him.

"Let's hear him out, Pops." He whispered.

The moment Mason saw Joey's face, he realized what he had forgotten to do. The last time Mason talked to Joey he told him he would let Blaire know about her past after a month. But he had forgotten to follow back up and feed him his lies. And because Joey had a new number due to trying to diss the people he used to use drugs with, nobody had gotten in contact with him. Including Spacey, Shay and Minnesota who were so busy living their own lives they lost touch with their brother.

Blaire, Joey and Preach stood in front of the table where the rest were seated.

Shay farted.

Mason rose and approached. Now he felt it was time to tell the truth. "Blaire, let me explain what—."

"Banks." She shrugged. "I mean, that's my real name right?" The pain in her eyes in that moment made Mason want to take the kitchen gun to his temple and end it all.

Besides, living without him would hurt just as badly.

"What you doing, unc?" Joey asked Mason shaking his head softly. He was playing SHAME, SHAME, SHAME, in his mind. "Why would you do my pops like this? I'm not understanding."

"I didn't mean to hurt her, I—."

"Him!" Blaire yelled. "My name is Banks Wales and I'm sick of your fucking lies!" He waved a fist in the air.

Mason paced a little and leaned against the fridge. His legs were so weak he could barely stand. The weight of his betrayal was crippling and yet it was his alone.

"We told him everything," Joey said. "You might as well tell the truth."

Mason held his head down. "I didn't want to lose you." He whispered. "I didn't want to lose us. And I'm so...I'm so..."

Minnesota sighed and Spacey rubbed her back. She was on the verge of a panic attack.

And seeing Mason break down even though he was dead wrong made everyone but Preach, Banks and Joey feel for him. It was evident that regardless of how foul his actions were, and they were wretched, losing Banks would be close to death.

"I knew something was wrong with me," Banks said in a low voice. "I knew something was wrong and you made me believe I was crazy." His eyes were red as tears fell down his cheeks. "You called me all kinds of dykes. Threatened to leave. And crushed my spirit every fucking day in this house. I don't remember anything about our past, but I need to know, what did I do in our time to make you treat me like this?"

Tears ran down Mason's face too. "I knew you were remembering, and I wanted to...to...hold onto you as long as possible."

"I'm crushed in ways I won't be able to come back from," Banks shook his head. "And it's all your fault. I'm learning that my whole world is a fucking lie." He looked at Minnesota. "And you...you're my daughter and you allowed this shit." He looked over at Spacey. "And you're my son." His eyes rested on Shay. "And even you betrayed me. How could all of you allow him to do this to me?"

Shay was shaken to her core. "Banks, please listen to me. I know I went along with this, whatever it is." She waved her hand toward Mason and the rest. Fully prepared to roll them under the bus if given the keys. "But I also was the one who never gave up on you. I was the one who kept asking everyone to find you. While they all gave up. Because I never wavered, even when Preach said you were dead."

Everyone looked at Preach. "I said you were dead, because your grandmother threatened me, Banks. And I needed her to help you because the other doctors that Mason hired were quacks and you were dying. And the only way she was going to help was if I said you were deceased. It was wrong but since you are alive I stand by my decision." His head rose higher.

"Banks, please," Shay continued. "Remember what you said in the kitchen when we were eating ice cream. You said you would remember me if I told you the truth."

"But you didn't though." Banks responded. "Preach and Joey told me."

"Exactly," Joey said. "Pops would've died for everybody in this room. And you choose to be disloyal?"

Minnesota fainted and Shay dropped to her knees to help as she came to. Spacey walked up to them too and sat on the floor.

"Blaire...I mean...Banks, did Preach and Joey tell you that you loved me?"

Banks didn't budge.

"I know you don't want to hear this, but you did love me. Everything that we experienced when we made love was real."

"Wrong time, pops." Derrick said shaking his head. "Wrong time."

"Just hear me out." Mason said to everybody. "Before your brain surgery, you were angry with me, Banks." He placed his hand over his heart. "Angry that I moved on and angry that I wasn't spending time with you."

"Nigga, this ain't it," Preach said swatting the air.

"I'm not talking to you!" He pointed at him. Focusing back on Banks he said, "You were jealous, so you killed a friend of mine. And you were going to confess how you felt about me but—"

Banks stepped in front of him. And everyone rose, as if he was the honorable Banks Wales.

But Mason continued to plead his case. "It's true."

"And that made you feel like I wanted to be dressed like a woman?" He glared. "Nigga, don't play games with me. I'm waking up now. I know all of this was about you."

Silence.

"Pops, I wanted to tell you, but they wouldn't let me." Shay said holding Minnesota in her arms. "They wouldn't let me do it!"

"But you didn't tell me though." He glared. "Did you?"

"I wanted to tell you too." Minnesota responded from the floor. "But Mason—."

"Minnesota, stop," Banks said. "I know you let Mason use your urine to convince me I was pregnant. And to hear that you and Spacey are my kids and you allowed...you allowed..." he shook his head and looked down. "And then Jersey." For this he stepped even closer and looked dead in Mason's eyes. "You had me deny my wife and take a bed with you instead. What kind of shit is this? What kind of people are you Louisville's?"

"Hold up, you never married that bitch!" Mason pointed at him. "It was never official." He looked at Joey and Preach. "And since they telling, did they tell you that she was my wife first? So, you tell me, who betrayed who? I may be wrong, but you are far from a martyr."

Banks stole him in the face, and he dropped. Derrick was about to go for the gun, but Mason raised a hand to stop him.

Licking the blood from his mouth he rose and said, "I'm sorry. But like I said, what about you? You're no more innocent then the rest of us. And if we are all crazy, you ran the asylum long before I did."

Banks stepped back and looked at all of them. "You right. All of this makes me wonder what kind of person Banks really was, to sleep with another man's wife. To raise children so terrible they would betray their *Pops*. And you know what..." he shrugged. "I don't know the answers. What I do know is that the only people I can trust in this room are at my side right now."

Joey and Preach stood taller.

"Don't try to find me." He looked at all of them. "You are all dead to me."

He turned to leave when Mason ran and got his gun, rushed up and grabbed Banks' hand. "Okay, what do you want? You want me to take my life?"

He put the gun at his head and cocked. "Just say the word!"

Preach aimed at Mason but Joey told him to hold off.

Mason got down on his knees as if he were proposing marriage to Banks all over again.

"Aw, pops, nah, it's over," Derrick said in total embarrassment. "Don't play yourself like this. He got on sweats! Blaire's gone!"

"Whatever you want me to do, I'll do." Mason said looking up at him. "Just please don't leave me."

"This nigga tripping," Preach said sighing.

"I don't remember you yet," Banks said softly looking down at him. "But I know I'll never trust you again. You just better hope that when I do remember, I won't want revenge." He snatched his hand away and walked out with Joey and Preach at his side.

Shay and Minnesota erupted in tears.

Later on, that night Mason walked into Morgan's room. He was a shell of a man. He looked torn up in a way she hadn't seen a person in a long time. His eyes were blood shot red and he smelled of alcohol and vomit combined. A mostly empty bottle of whiskey dangled from his paw.

Grabbing her robe, she placed it on and walked up to him as he hung in the doorway.

She could tell what he needed without words. Wrapping her arms around him she held him closely and said, "I'm here. It's okay. I'm here."

The bottle crashed to the floor as he wrapped his arms around her and wept in her arms. It was long. Hard. And necessary.

"Pops," Derrick said walking up behind them.

Mason released his hold, sniffled and tried to play tough. "What, nigga? You see I'm busy."

"Yeah okay, anyway, Dasher is here."

When Mason looked past him, Dasher was standing in the hallway holding their beautiful baby boy who she named, Bolt Louisville.

EPILOGUE

B anks sat on the deck outside of the villa that he rented in Costa Rica, alone. He was devastated and broken down emotionally in too many ways to count. The radio was playing but he wasn't listening.

Things had changed over the days he'd been there, and it was safe to say that the essence of Banks Wales was back.

His hair had been cut, revealing his short curly fro. And he traded his dresses for grey sweats, shorts and white t-shirts. And he was considering restarting hormone therapy, feeling as if that was the final piece missing in the puzzle of his life.

Although he didn't remember his past without the assistance of Joey and Preach, he did know he was more comfortable than he'd ever been by dressing male.

The sliding glass door opened. "Banks, are you ready?" Tinsley said walking out.

He looked back at him. "You know I don't even believe in this shit right?"

"I know. But there was a reason you wanted me to call her. Maybe that's all we need to know for now."

"So why should I do something I don't fully believe in?"

Tinsley walked outside and sat on a recliner across from him. With his eyes on the neon green beach he sighed. "When my mother was alive, she made a big deal about Santa Claus. It was truly her favorite holiday." He shook his head and laughed. "She loved it more than I did and I thought she was so cute when she would get so excited. Anyway, I knew there was no Santa Clause long before she officially told me."

Banks sat deeper into the chair.

"One day, my mother mistakenly took me to buy one of the toys, only to claim later that Santa gave it to me. And even though I knew Santa wasn't real, it still boosted my mood. It made me feel the essence of Christmas."

"So, what are you saying?"

"My hypnotist friend is good, Banks. Really good. But even if she doesn't help you remember all that you are, maybe you'll find your essence. And maybe that's all you need to do the rest."

He sighed having gotten his point loud and clear. "Maybe."

"I must say, you make a better, looking man than female. And that's saying a lot because you were drop dead gorgeous as a woman."

He shook his head. "I don't know who I am but I do know this feels right." He whipped a hand through his curls. "So where is everybody?"

"Joey and his wife are on the beach. And Preach's standing in the front of the door like he's protecting you from something. He said he's never leaving your side again." He laughed. "I keep telling him that Mason is nowhere near. And even if he was, I don't feel like he would hurt you. Now what he would do to me may be another story."

"He won't hurt you either." He glared.

"I wish that were true. But I heard him give the orders to take me out myself."

"Like I said, he won't touch you." He said firmer. "You have my word."

Tinsley hadn't felt that relieved since River.

"Although I know he's me, Banks seems to be a person with a lot of secrets. How else could he keep people like Mason around him? How else could he raise children like Minnesota, Spacey and Shay?"

"You're right." Tinsley nodded. "Oh, before I forget, your kids keep calling me. Guess they found out I'm with you. And Jersey too."

"I can't speak to them. Their commitment to the lie was too great to forgive."

"I understand. But they are still your family. At least talk to your wife."

"Leave it alone."

Tinsley nodded. "Respect."

"So, have you spoken to River?"

"You know, in my entire life I never had a friend like her. And I don't know if I ever will again. I just hope she understands that for some reason, I feel safer around you than back at home." He sighed. "I mean, she said she would talk to Mason about wanting me dead, but I saw his face when he gave the order. And I know how she feels about him. She feels like she owes him her life. So...so...how can I be sure she won't do what he intended from the gate? Even though the secret is out? Just because I'm with you."

"Who are these Lou and Wales people?" Banks asked.

"I wish I knew."

Banks sighed and stood up. "Tell your friend I'm ready to get started."

"Sure."

Tinsley walked back inside as Banks looked at the water. The whooshing noise it made was soothing as the song *Lately* by *Jodeci* played in the background.

For some reason, he immediately thought of Mason Louisville.

And so, he tossed the radio into the sea.

By T. STYLES

THE ELITE WRITER'S ACADEMY

Do you want to be financially secure?

Do you have an urban fiction book idea but don't know how to flesh it out?

Join our classes at
www.theelitewritersacademy.com

You'll receive access to past and future workshops!

Visit our website at
www.theelitewritersacademy.com

CARTEL PUBLICATIONS

PRESENTS

The Cartel Publications Order Form

www.thecartelpublications.com

Inmates **ONLY** receive novels for $10.00 per book **PLUS** shipping fee **PER BOOK.**
(Mail Order **MUST** come from inmate directly to receive discount)

Shyt List 1	_____	$15.00
Shyt List 2	_____	$15.00
Shyt List 3	_____	$15.00
Shyt List 4	_____	$15.00
Shyt List 5	_____	$15.00
Shyt List 6	_____	$15.00
Pitbulls In A Skirt	_____	$15.00
Pitbulls In A Skirt 2	_____	$15.00
Pitbulls In A Skirt 3	_____	$15.00
Pitbulls In A Skirt 4	_____	$15.00
Pitbulls In A Skirt 5	_____	$15.00
Victoria's Secret	_____	$15.00
Poison 1	_____	$15.00
Poison 2	_____	$15.00
Hell Razor Honeys	_____	$15.00
Hell Razor Honeys 2	_____	$15.00
A Hustler's Son	_____	$15.00
A Hustler's Son 2	_____	$15.00
Black and Ugly	_____	$15.00
Black and Ugly As Ever	_____	$15.00
Ms Wayne & The Queens of DC **(LGBT)**	_____	$15.00
Black And The Ugliest	_____	$15.00
Year Of The Crackmom	_____	$15.00
Deadheads	_____	$15.00
The Face That Launched A Thousand Bullets	_____	$15.00
The Unusual Suspects	_____	$15.00
Paid In Blood	_____	$15.00
Raunchy	_____	$15.00
Raunchy 2	_____	$15.00
Raunchy 3	_____	$15.00
Mad Maxxx (4th Book Raunchy Series)	_____	$15.00
Quita's Dayscare Center	_____	$15.00
Quita's Dayscare Center 2	_____	$15.00
Pretty Kings	_____	$15.00
Pretty Kings 2	_____	$15.00
Pretty Kings 3	_____	$15.00
Pretty Kings 4	_____	$15.00
Silence Of The Nine	_____	$15.00

By T. STYLES

Silence Of The Nine 2	_____	$15.00
Silence Of The Nine 3	_____	$15.00
Prison Throne	_____	$15.00
Drunk & Hot Girls	_____	$15.00
Hersband Material **(LGBT)**	_____	$15.00
The End: How To Write A	_____	$15.00
Bestselling Novel In 30 Days (Non-Fiction Guide)		
Upscale Kittens	_____	$15.00
Wake & Bake Boys	_____	$15.00
Young & Dumb	_____	$15.00
Young & Dumb 2: Vyce's Getback	_____	$15.00
Tranny 911 **(LGBT)**	_____	$15.00
Tranny 911: Dixie's Rise **(LGBT)**	_____	$15.00
First Comes Love, Then Comes Murder	_____	$15.00
Luxury Tax	_____	$15.00
The Lying King	_____	$15.00
Crazy Kind Of Love	_____	$15.00
Goon	_____	$15.00
And They Call Me God	_____	$15.00
The Ungrateful Bastards	_____	$15.00
Lipstick Dom **(LGBT)**	_____	$15.00
A School of Dolls **(LGBT)**	_____	$15.00
Hoetic Justice	_____	$15.00
KALI: Raunchy Relived	_____	$15.00
(5th Book in Raunchy Series)		
Skeezers	_____	$15.00
Skeezers 2	_____	$15.00
You Kissed Me, Now I Own You	_____	$15.00
Nefarious	_____	$15.00
Redbone 3: The Rise of The Fold	_____	$15.00
The Fold (4th Redbone Book)	_____	$15.00
Clown Niggas	_____	$15.00
The One You Shouldn't Trust	_____	$15.00
The WHORE The Wind		
Blew My Way	_____	$15.00
She Brings The Worst Kind	_____	$15.00
The House That Crack Built	_____	$15.00
The House That Crack Built 2	_____	$15.00
The House That Crack Built 3	_____	$15.00
The House That Crack Built 4	_____	$15.00
Level Up **(LGBT)**	_____	$15.00
Villains: It's Savage Season	_____	$15.00
Gay For My Bae	_____	$15.00
War	_____	$15.00
War 2: All Hell Breaks Loose	_____	$15.00
War 3: The Land Of The Lou's	_____	$15.00
War 4: Skull Island	_____	$15.00
War 5: Karma	_____	$15.00
War 6: Envy	_____	$15.00
War 7: Pink Cotton	_____	$15.00
Madjesty vs. Jayden (Novella)	_____	$8.99
You Left Me No Choice	_____	$15.00
Truce – A War Saga	_____	$15.00
Ask The Streets For Mercy	_____	$15.00
Truce 2 - The War of The Lou's	_____	$15.00

(Redbone 1 & 2 are **NOT** Cartel Publications novels and if <u>ordered</u> the cost is **FULL** price of $15.00 **each. No Exceptions.)**

TRUCE 2: THE WAR OF THE LOU'S   303

Please add **$5.00** for shipping and handling fees for up to **(2) BOOKS PER ORDER**. (INMATES INCLUDED) (See next page for details)

The Cartel Publications * P.O. BOX 486 OWINGS MILLS MD 21117

Name: _____

Address: _____

City/State: _____

Contact/Email: _____

Please allow 10-15 BUSINESS days Before shipping.

PLEASE NOTE DUE TO <u>COVID-19</u> SOME ORDERS MAY TAKE UP TO <u>3 WEEKS OR LONGER</u> BEFORE THEY SHIP

The Cartel Publications is <u>NOT</u> responsible for <u>Prison Orders</u> rejected!

<u>NO RETURNS and NO REFUNDS</u>
<u>NO PERSONAL CHECKS ACCEPTED</u>
<u>STAMPS NO LONGER ACCEPTED</u>